Dearest Pauline & Sean,

Thanks for all the fun & good times we have shared over the years. I hope you enjoy this spooky gothic tale of the ghostly Napoleon.

With love & best wishes,

Louise xxx

the story of an island,
an exile and an emperor

a novel by
Louise Hoole

BARRANCA PRESS

For my father and for St Helena,
both near and far.

What is the world, O soldiers?
It is I:
I, this incessant snow,
This northern sky;
Soldiers, this solitude
Through which we go
Is I.

'Napoleon'
by Walter de la Mare
(from *Poems*, 1906)

May 1821.

LOUISE HOOLE

1

I awoke that morning cool and calm, and when I touched my head I knew that the miracle had happened and that the fever had passed. In time, I moved a foot and felt the old heaviness gone. Gone, too, the strange cramps in my legs, the heat in my belly, the mustiness in my brain. I threw off the heavy blankets, and sat up.

My sight was as sharp as it had been when I was a young artillery officer. How I had rued the slow deterioration of my vision, and with what joy I celebrated its return! My hands were no longer stiff; I could smell citrus in the air; my mouth tasted bitter. In short, my senses were back.

I was immediately punished for the thought. Noises of the most atrocious volume assaulted my ears until I put my hands over my head and whimpered for them to stop. Random phrases screeched through the air. I heard Bertrand shouting: "You are wrong to do this, Sire!" and my own voice screaming back: "I was never wrong when I was Emperor. Then I was always right." There was a terrible sound like the clatter of a knife in a metal bowl or a hammer striking a nail. A bird call outside was like the blast of a cannon; a dog barking in the distance made me want to weep.

I tried to call out, but my own voice was so excruciating that I feared my eardrums would burst. A fresh assault of sound came from all around me, like that of a hundred men crying to be fed. The door to my bedroom swung open and for a moment Bertrand

1

appeared. I flapped my hands for him to approach, but he looked around the room as if searching for something, then went out. The slam, as he closed the door, was a crime.

I staggered to my feet, wrapped a pillow around my head, and forced myself to suffer the appalling pain of movement. The shriek of the doorknob as I turned it was like that of a man losing a limb.

As I entered the billiard room, the dreadful noises seemed to die down as quickly as they had begun. I closed my eyes, and clung for dark quiet moments of relief to the green-baize table. When I opened them again, I found myself looking down upon a body. I recognised immediately that it was my own.

It was my belly I recognised first. One doesn't live with one's abdomen for fifty-two years and not recognise it, even in a new, hard form. It was *my* belly: there was the point where flesh curled over flesh, a moist patch where red fungus grew; there were the maroon patches of the mustard plasters, the itching blisters intended to draw some sickness from me that were their own sickness; there was the mole from childhood, now, with age, sprouting five black hairs.

I did not fall to the floor; I did not stagger or faint. There was no light-headedness; the world did not spin. There was no urge to laugh or cry; my mind did not struggle to believe nor my eye to comprehend. I understood instantly and with absolute clarity: I was dead.

I stood without moving, and went on standing. Doors opened and people entered the room and there were snatches of conversation that I stored whole but unanalysed in my head. Yet I didn't do anything but stare and stare at my own belly, and when I looked at my abdomen it was with nothing but love and nostalgia, as I would have looked at an old friend suddenly gone. How I loved it in those moments – the belly that had caused me such pain in life! I loved its monumental size; the memory of its softness; even the small red fungus that had been a devil to me living, now only evoked the indulgence of an old enemy no longer worth engaging in a fight. I smiled as I looked at it, and the world seemed to burst into stars and meteorites and bright showery sparks of love. But when I reached out my hand to stroke the belly, it was hard and cold.

People moved around at the edges of my sight – mere shadows of dark and shade, black and mute. I could not have formed a sentence to speak, nor even to think. I was only sensation: sight and sound and taste and smell and touch.

There were sounds that entered my head that I can still remember and reproduce; there were the words 'God', 'Governor', 'Bertrand', 'the British', but they meant no more to me in those minutes than 'apple', 'orange' or 'string'. Everything was calm, peaceful and still, and I was filled with so much love for my old body that I could feel myself expanding with it: like a gourd or a goatskin I filled and filled, grew larger, expanded further, grew fantastically huge, stretching the membrane which enclosed me; the feeling was ecstatic, then excessive, then painful, and then – with a pop – the membrane exploded and was gone.

With the 'pop' everything changed. The feeling of calm vanished, pain returned, and there was a surge of anger. No, not anger. RAGE. I dragged my eyes from the belly and looked around. Outside, sheltering on the veranda, I saw Bertrand . . . I saw Gourgaud . . . Montholon . . . Marchand . . . I saw Fanny Bertrand smile. I saw the rain soaking the garden and the window shutters swinging, and inside the billiard room two English surgeons dressed in white aprons, arranging knives.

"This is not death," I said. "Where are the angels, the choirs, the white-robed figures, and the blond bearded man beckoning from a gate? Where is my father? Joséphine? General Ney? Where is the light?"

My leg shot out and kicked over a pail. There was a clatter, someone came running and the two surgeons looked up, nervous and surprised. "These are the last moments of consciousness," I told myself, "death is coming, oblivion is coming, the moment when everything is blank," and I was weeping, throwing up my arms, praying, laughing, shouting "I am here! . . . It is I!", but no one came for me, no one looked at me, no one said a thing.

I threw myself between the body and the two surgeons, and cried: "Stand away!"

But the Englishmen began instead to circle me.

"It is over!" I shouted, "Enough!", but their eyes were fixed on my old body, and in a moment the tall one lowered his face and began to sniff around my neck. I watched with astonishment as his nostrils dilated and flared, hovered around my face and ears like an insect, sniffing along the length of my legs and arms, circling my belly button, my groin, my feet.

"I thought there was something strange," he said finally.

"Lavender?"

"Yes, I think so. Someone has smeared the corpse with scent."

"Irritating."

"Yes."

Watching, I felt insubstantial, light as a puff of down, airy like a spider's web, blown around in the wind.

"Why the billiard table?"

"It was the only surface on which he would fit."

"And they always said he was so short!"

"But not small."

"No. Not small."

"Let us call in the others."

"One moment . . . " the taller one said.

I placed myself between them and my body. "What is this? What outrage . . . ," but the short one turned to his companion and said,

"Is it General Bertrand who has agitated for this?"

The other nodded. "He was most insistent. Insistent, too, that all the French should be here."

"Even the woman?"

"Even the servants." He raised his eyes incredulously. "He insists there should be as many French witnesses as possible. Bonaparte shouted so often that he was being murdered that the French have come to believe it."

They laughed.

A great hush fell over my mind as I heard their words. "It is a dream," I told myself. "A man who dies without a confessor is a fool, and I have not confessed."

"Tell the others they may come in."

I looked at the body on the table - whose chest did not rise and fall - and then down at the feet I could still move, and my mind was battered with new terrors. For in this cleave between life and death I saw no light drawing me towards a new life; I found no mystery finally revealed; there was no God, no heaven, and yet also no oblivion and no forgetfulness.

"Transition," I called out shakily, trying to rise to the occasion. "Present yourself! Let the end come. Let there be finality."

But still nothing changed.

A flood of people had begun pouring into the room when I finally understood that my mind had separated from my body, and that, if I wanted them to re-join, I must decisively assist them to do so. There was nothing for it but to climb upon the table, and lay myself over - or rather on, in, on top of, identically positioned with - that body which was so familiar. I took pains to walk around my courtiers whom I recognised, and the men in white aprons whom I did not, and placing my knee on the high corner of the billiard table, I pulled myself onto it and, with a shudder of distaste, allowed my moving body to merge with the prone body as it lay there on the sheet.

5

I closed my eyes and emptied my mind of thought. I tried to think of words as pure sound, empty of meaning, and since there was English and French in the room as well as the singsong sound of Italian, I allowed the languages of Europe to merge. I separated the other sounds: the clattering of metal from threads being cut, shuffling of feet and coughing, a sob from a corner, the clattering of a pail, a scraping of a quill on stiff parchment. I believed that if I could identify the noises without interpreting them, my mind would have that small but necessary activity that would allow it to move into a trance. In an altered state, the transition would surely come, for nothing could happen while I was lucid and sharp, taut with awareness, and only just keeping my horror at bay.

But of a sudden, there was a disturbance, the sound of a door opening and slamming, and it was followed by the familiar voice of Bertrand announcing flatly, without a trace of a flourish: "His Excellency, the Governor, Sir Hudson Lowe."

The words came into my head, but I tried not to think what they meant. I continued with my list of sounds - separating this from that - and I succeeded for a little while, until it became obvious from the warm stinking breath above me that someone was looking down on me and that they were very close.

I opened my eyes. I hadn't seen him for five years, and then only thrice, but nothing could erase that scaly freckled skin, that sparse red hair and those fish-like eyes from my mind. He looked at me with an aspect of pure hate. For a moment, the surprise of having my face and my jailor's so close that we might swap air, stuck me to the table in a paralysis of shock. What was Old Feather-Brain doing looking down upon me so intently? He looked as if he wanted to whip me. And I, in my weakened state and prone position, felt powerless to command him to stand away.

Before my opened eyes, Lowe straightened up. He turned to Bertrand and asked: "Can you confirm it is Bonaparte?"

"It is the Emperor," Bertrand said.

Lowe took a large breath, as if the discovery had exhausted him. Then he coughed, drew himself up, and said: "The death of General Bonaparte is a tragedy for both his family and friends." Then he turned on his heel, and, with a stiff back, as if he could feel my eyes boring into his behind, he stiffly left the room.

It took me a moment to recover. Lowe's repulsive face was not what one would have wished for in those lonely moments. But as I was resolving to close my eyes again and regain my trance, another voice broke in on me: it was Bertrand's, and it was very harsh.

"Ready now, Antommarchi," he said, and I saw the damn fool doctor, who had not been able to keep me alive, nod and pick up a knife.

A lesser man than I would have fled at that very moment, and there has been no man greater. I acknowledge that I was weakened – I have always been able to level criticism at my state – but even I found it difficult to go on lying there with that fat, white fool glinting his rings and blades at me, and looking at me in such a rapacious manner. You would think my body was a plump pigeon for all the greed with which he came, brandishing his knife, towards it.

A silence fell over the room. The surgeons in white shuffled nearer to the table, and there were so many of them, and they came so suddenly and so close, that for a moment the whiteness of their aprons duped me, and I thought that I was indeed travelling towards the light. Then, when they were closer still, I saw that it was only Antommarchi and seven unmistakably English surgeons, and behind them – on tip toes, or peeping between their heads – the faces of my generals, my servants and my priest. A lesser man, as I have said, would have fled before me, but when I snapped my fingers before their noses and there was no response, I removed myself with some urgency from the table.

What has distinguished me from my fellow men, time and again, is the speed with which I adapt: those Frenchmen were still harping on about republics, when I had seen that the time was ripe for an emperor; religion was still the enemy to them, when I restored the faith to its people.

During my exile, nothing had happened. St Helena had brought no novelty of circumstance, no dashing escapes. In our shrunken existence, the slaughter of a sheep excited as much interest as my annihilation of the Prussians had once done in France. On the island there was nothing but squabbling and fighting over trifles, played out daily in our too-small house. Not since I was a young artillery officer waiting for destiny and reading Werther had I been so crushingly bored: I felt as if I were chained before an untextured white wall. Before my men I controlled myself impeccably – they should hardly have known that I rued what had come to pass. But in the night, on my own, I paced my room perpetually and screamed silently for change, any change.

Now, at last, the turn of fortune that I had prayed for was upon me, and I took what it offered with grasping hands. Once I realised that my body was about to be cut up, I felt no pity for it. Nostalgia and faintheartedness left me, and I was filled only with curiosity. After all, it could hardly fail to interest me, the cause of my own demise.

I had now taken up a position opposite Antommarchi, between two of the English surgeons, and from there I could see Generals Montholon and Gourgaud, and to their left Bertrand and Fanny. Father Vignali had moved to sit by one of the windows, and the servants - Marchand and Pierron - to stand at attention by the interior and exterior door. Marchand looked strained, and his skin was grey with fatigue.

"I am sorry for your loss," the tall English surgeon said to Bertrand.

"Merci, Dr Chapman."

"And for the loss of all your party," he said with a glance that took in all my courtiers.

"Merci encore."

"The Governor has told you of my role?"

"He has informed me that you will lead the post-mortem and that Dr Antommarchi will only assist."

Antommarchi coughed and moved towards Chapman. "It was the Emperor's wish," he said in pompously precise but heavily accented English, "that there should be a post mortem and that a detailed report of it should be conveyed to his son. It was his wish that I alone should look inside him. He left *express instructions* to that effect."

"I am sorry to disappoint you."

"We understand," Bertrand said gravely, "that it is neither your decision, nor your fault."

Chapman nodded, then inclined his head towards the window. "It is . . . er . . . an unpleasant day for such a thing."

For a moment all eyes turned to look at the rain battering the window. A shutter that had come loose banged in the wind and its clatter reverberated through the thin wooden walls of the house.

"The days at Longwood are always unpleasant," Bertrand said quietly, "but I imagine you are not here to talk about the weather."

"No, indeed." Chapman looked around the green-papered room for a moment, taking in the tiny fireplace, the small mirror, the miniatures on the wall. Then he turned his gaze to the billiard table, on which my yellowed body was lying.

"Light the candles, will you," Chapman asked one of the English surgeons. "Place them at the head and foot of the table."

He opened his bag with a snap and began arranging his instruments on the table.

"He died this morning, Dr Antommarchi?"

9

"At nine minutes to six."

"The cadaver has not been touched since?"

"Not even to be washed. As you asked."

"Good." Chapman made some minute adjustments to his instruments, then looked up with an expressionless face and addressed the surgeons.

"This is science, gentlemen," he said in his quiet English voice. "Not guess work. We shall ignore all that we have heard of Bonaparte's illnesses in the island taverns at night. You know the tales, you have heard the rumours . . . that Bonaparte has been killed by wind and rain, by ennui and indignity and despair. We ourselves, as men of *science*, will not find that the wind or rain are to blame, for men don't die of wet weather, nor for that matter of *poison of the soul*. Inside the cadaver we shall find our answer, and our search shall take us towards the sublime. For how does it come about, we shall ask, this wearing down of the body, this shutting down?"

He put down the cloth and moved around the table self-consciously, like an actor playing a role. He nodded at Antommarchi who handed him a blade. He crossed himself with the scalpel and then, resting its cutting edge upon my chest, said: "Very well, gentlemen, since the Governor has seen him, we shall start."

The first incision: a long flourish along the swollen belly of my body. My skin parted, just a little, and balls of yellow-brown fat appeared to either side of the knife. He made another long, slow, shallow pass along my hairless abdomen, and then a third, exquisitely controlled, sweeping slice along the same line. With each movement of the knife nothing was revealed, but further depths of yellow fat. The surgeons, splayed around the table, looked in wonder at my larded belly.

One said: "Such corpulence is quite remarkable after so long an illness."

But Chapman did not reply.

Antommarchi was hunched over the table following the movement of his knife with feverish eyes. I could see that he approached my dead body with more joy than he had ever approached me alive, his eyes ablaze with his love of the inside. It seemed as if it was a relief to him no longer to have a patient following his eyes. Now he could stare without embarrassment, just as he had always wished, taking in the glabrous, monumental belly, the hairless testicles, the fatty pads over my chest like a woman's breasts.

More strokes followed along the incision site, never deeply, nor impatiently – just a slow working apart of the globules of fat.

"Ah, yes!" Chapman exclaimed as his final cut revealed the cavity of the abdomen with its merry pink organs, nestling side by side. He reached for the bowel, and began pulling it out, piling its python-like bulk over the abdomen and chest and groin.

Bertrand's face was pale and grey: he looked as if he might faint with shock. Bertrand – who had once been a fine soldier, who had seen so much – petrified by the calm voice of a doctor saying "large bowel" or "small bowel" as he pulled out pieces of pink flesh.

I saw Bertrand take Fanny's arm to steady himself, and Montholon let out a sigh.

On my torso, the still bowel sat, the bowel that in life would have been pulsating pinkly, moving, glistening and shining with its network of blue marbled veins. The pale, thin hands of Chapman marked a single spot on the organ with a yellow-tasselled pin. This was his starting point. And from it he drew each part of the bowel through his hands, turning and twisting, and peering closely at all the curves of its cylindrical walls.

When he had finally satisfied himself, he pronounced: "No abnormalities observed, either on the large or small bowel."

I saw the amanuensis, an English officer sitting at my own desk, write this down.

With five sharp slices of his scalpel, Chapman detached the bowels from the abdominal wall and moved their slippery bulk to the bottom of the table, leaning them against the imperial feet. The torso without the cover of bowels had a monstrous look. The flesh to either side of the incision line sagged and wrinkled, like an unbuttoned jacket. It gave my body a peculiarly slovenly look.

"Dr Antommarchi, if you would."

Chapman and Antommarchi positioned themselves on either side of the chest and pulled apart the flesh shirt until it was stretched and taut. Then, with surgical clips, they pinned the rolls of fat to either side of the flanks.

"The soup ladle, if you please."

Antommarchi handed it to him and held out the jug. I watched the ladle curve into my abdomen, scoop, and come out brim-full of blood. Then it went in again.

"There has been a haemorrhage," Chapman said. "How much is that?"

"One-sixth of a gallon," Antommarchi replied. "And there's more. It is recent. Fresh."

"Yes."

Chapman selected a small saw and carved out a triangular section from the front wall of the chest. As he did so, the remaining flesh moved and vibrated beneath his touch. He put the portion of bone down beside the feet and bowel, then straightened himself up.

"Now, let's have a closer look."

He prodded a few organs and said: "The stomach is adhered to the wall of the liver."

With a few expert slashes he severed the two organs from the abdominal cavity, and held them up. The surgeons exchanged professional nods.

"There is extensive inflammation of the stomach, and a perforation is visible one inch above the pylorus. What do you think, Antommarchi? Come and have a closer look." He dangled the organ before him like he might an apple to a horse.

I leant forward to catch his words, to see if I had been right.

"The stomach's wall is corroded and there is a hole in it . . . ," he put his finger through the hole, "the size of a man's little finger. The internal surface is viscous, pitted like a honeycomb, and filled with cells of dark coloured pus."

He looked up and nodded grimly at the other surgeons.

"It is a cancer. The Emperor would have succumbed to the disease on the throne of France as well as on St Helena. Had the liver not adhered to the stomach wall, he would almost certainly have died sooner. The liver acted as a stopper, if you like, sealing the matter of the stomach into its own cavity, rather than allowing it to escape into the peritoneum." He looked down at the organ and sliced casually through a few layers. "I believe he has been affected by the same lesion that brought his father to the grave. It was, as we know, always his own fear."

It was true. I *had* once said that cancer was the matter with me; that it was my hereditary fault. When I first began vomiting, I could not help but talk of a tumour, the very sort from which I had seen my father suffer. But after a time, when it was clear what was happening and what was going to happen, I had changed my plaint.

I watched Antommarchi with contempt: the punctilious way he was packing the detached stomach in a silver pepper dish, and covering the poor organ with French brandy. He approached the task with an assiduity I had rarely witnessed before then. Had he been as careful with my live self, as he was with my corpse, I might actually have survived.

Chapman clicked his tongue, picked up a new object from the mess of entrails before him and proclaimed: "The liver, on the other hand, is normal."

Antommarchi swung his head round, peered closely and then cried: "No, Dr Chapman! I cannot allow that. The liver is clearly enlarged!"

"The liver is, as I say, quite normal."

"That is an enlarged liver, sir. There is an inflammation of the organ, a hepatitis!"

"There is a difference," explained Chapman, as if he were talking to a child, "between a liver that is *large*, and an *enlarged* liver. This is certainly for a man of Bonaparte's size" – and here he allowed himself to raise a sardonic eyebrow – "a large liver, but I cannot have it that it is enlarged, by which one would conclude that it was diseased. There is no disease here."

"What shall I write for the record, sir?" asked the officer at the desk. "Is it diseased or not?"

"Please, gentlemen," cried the Governor's aide-de-camp stepping forward "try and agree. General Bonaparte has put it about that this is an unhealthy island, riddled with hepatitis and disease, that the life of a European is consumed here in a few years, and that the English in bringing him to St Helena are responsible for his death. His claims are upheld or rejected by your report. Therefore, I beg you to look at the organ again and come to a conclusion that is unanimous. The peace of Europe," he ended grandiosely, "may depend upon it."

"Gorrequer," said Chapman irritably. "You speak as if we were imbeciles. We should hardly be in this room if we were unaware of those facts."

Gorrequer blushed, and stepped back.

Two drops of perspiration rolled down Chapman's brow, slid along his nose and fell into the pink cavity below. Commanding the room's attention, he held up the liver in the air and slashed through it.

"Look! The liver is healthy. See! Perhaps it *is* a little inflamed by me dragging it from the stomach on which it was stuck, but . . . ."

"That would not affect the organ after death!" Antommarchi interrupted, his face growing very red. "The liver is enlarged in all probability because this island is tropical and wet – the very worst conditions for disease. One need only observe the high incidence of hepatitis amongst the English troops to see what happens to the European physique here."

"The soldiers' lifestyle is to blame," said Chapman angrily. "They drink too much, because they have nothing to do. There have been three thousand of them to guard a sick man!"

He paused and looked around the room. His voice was low and dangerous as he said: "There is no hepatitis here. This liver is quite healthy. But, what if there was a hepatitis; what if there was? Is this the fault of the English; is it proof of murder? Have you a hepatitis, General Bertrand or you Madame? Have I, or His Excellency, Sir Hudson Lowe?"

"Hudson Lowe has been lucky enough to live in a less rainy part of the island, whereas this is the island's most wretchedly wet plateau."

"There is hardly more rain here than in Bournemouth," Chapman remarked with a smile and the English surgeons laughed.

Antommarchi's face twisted in derision. "I suppose that most climates seem wonderful to the English. On the other hand, the French were born to expect more from the weather, and those from Corsica still more so. They say that the English sun is not equal to the Corsican moon. Is that not so, Comte Bertrand?"

But Bertrand did not answer, for in truth the argument was a pathetic one. Not even I had really hoped that Europe would believe me murdered by wet weather. When one starts to *insist* on theories like these, everything is lost.

Chapman stepped nearer to the table, menacing the shorter Antommarchi with his height. "Is it so impossible to accept that a man like him has died? That his body – just like everyone else's – is a machine for living that runs only a certain length of time?"

"He was fifty-two when he died," Antommarchi said coldly. "Close to your age, I should imagine."

"Every lifetime has its own ordained span."

Chapman looked at Antommarchi impatiently. "Had England wanted to kill him, she might easily have done so. She might have stood him up against the wall and shot him when he first surrendered, as he undoubtedly would have done to Wellington had the situation been reversed. Instead, she has spent a great deal of money and has gone to a great deal of trouble to keep him alive and comfortable here. It doesn't make sense," he shook his head in exasperation. "Why should England choose to kill him slowly?"

Antommarchi grew very pale. "It is not for me to say why the English acted or didn't act as they did. It is only for me to point out what I find before me, and to say whether he died of causes in which the English are implicated. There has been an ulceration of the stomach, and there is an enlargement of the liver. The two symptoms together are significant, the second casting a doubt on the conclusions I drew from the first. Since the liver is the processor of toxins, poisons to the body –"

"The liver is unremarkable," Chapman interrupted. "General Bonaparte died of a cancer of the stomach, nothing more."

The argument went on for a while, and then died down. I didn't listen to the rest, for my eyes kept catching those of my son, looking down at me from his portrait on the wall.

"Is there anything more you can do for me?" he seemed to be asking with his innocent blue eyes. "Have you done everything you could?"

"My plan is in progress," I answered him, "even now. Even now the news of my martyrdom is warming your throne. Everything will come to pass as I have intended .... You, my son, will soon be the second jewel in the Bonaparte crown."

I believe I must have gone on to say a great deal more, because when I dragged my eyes from my son's and once again became aware of the room, I saw that the candles had burnt down an inch, and that my oesophagus, spleen, bladder, kidneys, tongue and heart had been thrown into a pile at my feet.

"Now the brain," Chapman announced, resting a caressing hand on my dead man's head. I saw him trace the back of his blade around the outline of my face, along my hairline, and across the jaw: and knew that it was skin and scalp that he would love to pull back. He alone looked in fine form; he alone was not bridled with reverence for me. He possessed only the respect of the anatomist towards the corpse that enlightens him, and I confess that in those moments I rather admired his vigour.

"Not the brain," Bertrand said softly, shaking his head. "Not the brain."

But Chapman silenced him with a lofty movement of the hand, and said: "General Bertrand, I am afraid you do not honour the Emperor. The state of this organ in a man such as His Majesty would be of the greatest interest."

Then, when he could see his words had not moved him, he added: "Is it not you yourself who have so often spoken of his mental suffering on St Helena? Since the depressing passions of his mind, given a propensity towards predisposition, may have acted as an exciting cause of his death, I must, in respect of my honourable profession, insist on an examination of this organ."

But it was Baron Gourgaud who answered him, with his usual hysteria, with flapping hands and a flushed face. His voice was shrill and unpleasant as he half-shouted, half-said: "The Emperor's suffering was incomparable. It is my opinion that his tethering on St Helena animated the misery that ate away his stomach. But can you find wretchedness? Can we see it in the brain and label it? We have found the secondary cause: the cankerous stomach. The rest must be left to the conscience of the English. The Emperor must keep the mystery of his genius to himself."

Then, when Chapman went to speak again, Gourgaud shrieked: "You stand over his cadaver, pulling out and holding forth viscera, like a butcher calling his wares."

Chapman withdrew his blade from my head, and turned to face him with unconcealed distaste.

"Baron Gourgaud – "

But Gourgaud could no longer control himself and instead called for scissors. Scissors! Scissors were *necessary*! Were *imperative*! For Baron Gourgaud must have a piece of hair! He called for those scissors with the hysteria of a man who is taking leave of the person to whom he feels he has dedicated his whole life. In such a moment, my hair was everything to him. My hair, at that hour, was a castle or a continent for which he would fight.

"Marchand," said Fanny Bertrand in a quiet voice, "Please fetch my sewing scissors from our house. They are in the drawing room, beside my tapestry."

Marchand bowed and left.

The atmosphere in the room settled and stillness descended. The surgeons made no attempt to cut open the brain, nor to reunite my organs with my abdomen, nor to tie the stitches that should have held me together. On the contrary, they, like my courtiers, stood stock still, as if silhouettes frozen on a frieze.

A horrid foreboding came over me. During the autopsy, I had been sustained by my natural interest in the diagnosis of my illness. The thing from which I had suffered for two years and more could hardly fail to interest me. But of a sudden the examination was over, and with its cessation I looked at my flesh again, not now with the professional interest of a doctor seeking a fault, but with the nostalgia of a man for his old casing, perfect or not.

I looked at myself lying there with a tear up my middle, and my pulled apart chest emptied of organs. There were scars from the blisters and mustard plasters that ran intermittently from my collar to my feet. My stomach was on the sideboard marinating in brandy, and my sliced-up heart was splayed upon the table, waiting to be packed in a silver sponge dish and sent to my wife.

The wait for Marchand seemed interminable. Gourgaud cursed him "as a blasted servant who has gone to pieces," and even I myself felt a certain anger with him for leaving me there. I tried not to look at the body on the table, to busy myself with the portrait of my son, or the one of Marie-Louise that hung on the opposite wall. I swung my head to the left and then to the right, but my eyes kept returning to the thing in-between. And I realised, with a terror quite fresh to me, that I was no longer a pink and healthy man – an Emperor with a crown and a thinking brain – but a man with an empty space in his abdomen; a hard, cold, yellow, dead thing, beginning to turn waxy and marmoreal. My old body was nothing more than a chaos of entrails, blood, mucus and organs splayed across the table and splattering minutely on the floor.

2

My body was not embalmed despite what I had decreed. They might have done it. They might have used sulphur or coal tar, gunpowder or arsenic, even common salt. At the time I thought my men had forgotten my orders in the drama of the day, and I did not once suspect that some of those present – for reasons of their own – wanted my body to decompose so that it was not left for the curious eyes of an inquiring future.

But preservation of another sort went on. My generals took out their sketchbooks to try to preserve a final image, though I doubt it was the one burned on their brains. They didn't sketch me with my bowels hanging out, or with Chapman dangling my large liver in the air. Instead, Bertrand traced in white chalk on black paper the outline of my head, and Montholon drew my bloated body resting – not on a billiard table – but on an imagined imperial bed. Gourgaud tried to take an impress of my gaunt face with soggy paper, which was not, unsurprisingly, a success.

And there was thievery beyond the snatching of this final image. Marchand came back at last with sharpened scissors, and I watched as French and English men queued up to snip off clumps of my sparse chestnut hair.

As I watched them shearing off my locks, I thought of the shoddy series of events that had brought me here. Was it really possible that my surrender to the British had brought me to this? That they should have betrayed me so vilely, banished me from Europe, sent me to this tiny island at the other end of the earth? Provided living conditions so far below that which an Emperor, even a fallen emperor, might expect? That fall: from sitting in ermine, ruling Europe – the hugeness of those palaces, that space – to this tiny island and house; from a court of thousands to be left with three dullard generals, two old servants, a woman, a doctor and a priest.

I thought of the last six years. Six years . . . a footnote in the book of my life, a footnote of ignominy and nothingness; a footnote in which mastery – lacking throne, ermine, jewels, space – was so hard to maintain. I had once told my brother: "Everything that is vast is great. One can ignore many defects in the immense." But how can one ignore the defects in the miniscule?

As if to prove my point, Montholon and Gourgaud had begun to bicker over how the lid of the silver sponge box, which held my heart, could best be soldered. I looked around my court with anger. Still the same petty squabbles and sordid disputes, the bubbling private disappointments that they had never – courtly etiquette aside – tried to keep from me. I had told them time and again their rank and order: Count Bertrand, Grand Marshal of the Imperial Palace; Marquis Montholon, Head of the Household Stores; Baron Gourgaud, aide-de-camp. But it was like living with a bunch of unruly children, and all their arguments, however inconsequential, were referred to me.

That day, as I stood watching, I believed I was familiar with betrayal. Not just that of the British, but betrayal by my own family. It was still painful to remember that none of them had offered to share my exile, and that I – who had won the crowns of Europe and shared them amongst my siblings – had been abandoned by them in my shame. Even my wife, Marie-Louise, had ignored my pleas to come, and had stayed resolutely with her Austrian parents, keeping from me, most agonisingly of all, my French son.

Chapman had begun cutting the autopsy sheet into squares, and was now distributing to the surgeons these little, cold, linen squares splattered with my entrails. I wished I had not seen the little chips of rib that Antommarchi removed with his scalpel, or the small piece of stomach that he surreptitiously cut off and slipped - whilst others were consumed with their own covetousness - inside the black bag at his feet.

As I stood there, shocked and slow, I thought: *Perhaps I should be glad it's all over, glad that finally there is an end.* How little I knew then! How far was I from understanding that death would not be the end of what happened to me on St Helena, that it was only the beginning? That in the days that followed I would begin to discover, slowly, falteringly - ignoring what was significant, obsessed by what was not - layer upon layer of betrayal; betrayals that would lead me to an understanding more awful than any I could have imagined; betrayals that threatened to destroy everything for which I had worked. I ask myself, why did I not see it then? And I answer myself: Because nobody but the perpetrator *could* have seen.

The organs that had been dissected were swept with one firm movement of the hand into a bucket, which later Marchand - weeping, praying - would bury in the forest behind Longwood. Then they began to stuff my emptied abdomen with straw. And as Antommarchi began to sew the catgut knots that would tie me together, the trance of passivity left me, and with my arms outstretched before me, I fled in holy terror from that room.

3

When I fled from the autopsy room, I fled from awareness, I sought oblivion, I held out my arms to endings, to forgetfulness. I ran from the billiard room out into the ornamental garden and flung myself into the ha-ha at its deepest, deepest point, because I wanted a suitable burial; I wanted to bury the body that no-one else could see.

Lying flat at the bottom of my sunken path, I was comforted by the fairy terns whirling above, by the smell of gorse and pine, and from being held - as it seemed at the time - in the grassy arms of the earth. At first, the sounds of the house came to me: a door opening, a raised voice. But in time, Longwood House and the little ramshackle village of sheds, cows and outhouses scattered to the north became quiet. For years there had been processions of officials, shouts and loud arguments that broke out like winds, the frenzy of too many people too close. Now, not wishing to hear the soft sounds that told me it was over, I put my hands over my ears. Voices still murmured through the air, but I didn't look up and I tried not to listen, but to focus with all my might on the clouds and sky-changes until the worst had passed. For I would not think of my old body being attended with ceremony, while I lay on the ground in a ditch.

Despite my efforts to forget, my mind nagged constantly at the past. Scenes from my dying days came back to me with a vividness that astonished me, as if I were living them again, as if there were something in them I had sworn not to forget.

Two months I had lain dying in that bed by the wall, the sheets moist around me, my head hot, my feet cold. I had lain dying for two months, since March the 13th. But I had been ill before that. How long? Two years? Yes. Perhaps. I had been dying for two years.

There had been respites from my illness, times when I could get up and walk in the garden, leaning on Marchand's arm, or take a little nourishment of the usual kind. But mostly I had been fed on milk jellies and thin soups, which my valet had pushed into me spoon by spoon.

Each day my body changed in small but peculiar ways, and whilst my face and calves became thinner and thinner, the rest of my body – despite the fact that I was eating virtually nothing – became fatter and fatter. I could see my courtiers looking at me in astonishment. And the doctors, when I swore that I had eaten nothing for months, nodded their heads wisely and took it for a lie. For none of them could explain why it was that I ate nothing and grew larger.

"Medicine kills more men than it saves," I heard myself say, as fever crept slowly upon me.

"I do not fear death, but I will do nothing to hasten it," I told the doctors as they held their leeches before me, begging to let them suck. Then they dangled potions and I said, "I will not grasp at straws," but then I was too weak to prevent them and they swarmed over me, held me down and applied their suckers. I was covered with hungry leech mouths, with mustard plasters, with boiling cups. There was not a moment at which they weren't begging me to eat something, vomit something, pass something.

"Purge, vomit, suck," I asked them breathlessly. "Is that it? Is that all medicine has to offer?"

They smiled with condescension when I said I would drink only a little watered down wine: "If it does me no good, it will yet do me no harm. You doctors treat me like a bull, but my body needs delicate things; I am like the elephant that will balk at a rope, but be led by a string."

"These medicines are very mild, Your Majesty! They are the sort of thing one gives to a child."

"It would not take a cannon ball to kill me, a grain of sand would suffice."

The doctors tut-tutted. "It is true Your Majesty is weak, but we have seen patients who were a great deal more sick recover. You must have hope!"

"You physicians would promise life to a corpse if it could swallow your pills. These are just words! Words for women and children! Doctors should speak the truth to men, especially those who have been soldiers."

"We have told you the truth," they replied. "We have said what we think."

"Tomorrow then, what will be best? Some medicine or some soup?"

"Calomel without any doubt . . . if the intestines are opened, the condition of the stomach will improve."

I dismissed the doctors. "I perceive you have no means of curing me."

"The tongue is good," I heard them whispering as they moved away. "But we must strengthen his stomach. A few spoonfuls of vermicelli, some sieved sorrel and a mouthful of puréed partridge. Tomorrow he may have a little toast soaked in wine."

"Very soon I shall not even be able to piss without everyone talking about it," I called out.

They turned and looked at me.

"I have not made a will yet," I shouted. "If I die now, no-one will get a thing."

Then, turning to dear Marchand: "Chase away the flies, my friend."

As I lay dying, there were periods of light and periods of dark; there were human voices, and there was birdsong. And punctuating all this were drinks and drafts and potions. "Try the orgeat, Sire," they said. "The almonds have just arrived from France . . . . Try a little watered-down wine. Some liquorice water? A milk jelly?" Then: "Take your medicines, Majesty. Just another mouthful, just one more sip before sleep."

They knew, in truth, they knew *potions* wouldn't cure me, and I knew, I certainly knew. But since I had once been Master of Europe, they fought my dying to the very end. I was allowed no resignation to my fate. No humble acceptance or preparation for the time. Everyone told me that I would soon recover, or shouted in my ear: Fight! Fight! Fight!

As I lay dying, my courtiers came to whisper to me, one after the other. Sometimes they thought I was awake and sometimes they thought I was asleep, but they would unburden themselves upon me - *upon me!* - as if I didn't have enough burdens of my own as I lay there rueing what had come to pass. "Keep it to yourself," I tried to say, but the words didn't come out properly. "I beg your pardon, Majesty," they said bending their ears towards me, with an exaggerated look of listening. Then when I tried again, they pressed my head back on the pillow and murmured: "Rest now . . . rest."

I had no power to silence them any more or keep them away. I wanted to command them to find me handsome, to find me lean and trim, but they found me to be just what I was: a fat old man dying in a bed, far from home. Only Marchand was able to conquer his distaste in a way that the others could not, in a way that only women are usually able. And he called forth from his heart a generosity of spirit in which he bathed my last months.

I wanted Marchand, but the others would insist. They would sit
out the nights with me, those last long horrible nights, saying, "Just
one more mouthful, Your Majesty, just another sip," and moving
me less often than I wished. I don't know why they wanted to sit
with me and I feared them, for as my spirit faded, their power grew.
And I did not like what some of them were becoming, and I did
not like the fact that my will had now been made, and I was no
longer strong enough to change it.

How guilelessly I trusted them! How completely I expected them
to behave just as I had decreed: "You must return to France when
I die and work for my brothers. You will not marry amongst the
English. You will never work for a Bourbon king."

Their faces had grown pale. "Majesté! Non! Bien sûr que non!"

"Take these documents when you go; hide them in the lining of
your waistcoats. They contain everything my son needs to aban-
don Austria and recover the throne of France."

All this in a moment of lucidity. Bows and kind looks.

"Majesty, we will always obey your every command."

But it seems they had not.

I began drifting from people so that they said I was losing my
mind. I did have fevers. I did have deliriums in which I was far
away from the world, but at other times I came to with great clarity, and the things that I saw shocked me. The way people spoke
of 'Bonaparte' around my bed as if I was not there, as if I were no
longer 'the Emperor'. The way they began dividing up my things:
I could see them doing it, though they spoke in codes in front of
me. All trying to absolve themselves from blame – insisting they
had never wished to leave me on St Helena, that they had always
intended to see me through to the very end. All hoping for a claim
in the will . . . no, that's wrong . . . not all.

27

In the ha-ha, long shadows had passed across me and the lilac haze of twilight had arrived without my noticing. Noises, I suppose, went on but unheard, and I wasn't sure whether I was asleep or awake, and I didn't ask myself which I was because that would beg the question of whether I would ever sleep, or eat, or drink, or make love again, now that my bodily needs had gone.

As I lay there in the dusk among the agapanthus and ornamental paths, did I ask myself why I had died when the Bourbons were having difficulties in France? When a wave of nostalgia for my reign was gaining strength? No. I was an exile and knew nothing of these things. Did I ask why, after a slow two-year decline, the final dispatch – the lightning flash of death – had caught me by surprise? Again, I did not. Perhaps these questions would have arisen had I lain longer in the ha-ha, but at some point a voice broke in on me and it was a voice that I recognised from some seemingly dim past. "Where are you now?" it seemed to say. "What are you now?" And of a sudden it grew louder, and clearly said, "You bastard!" And opening my eyes without meaning to, I saw an elegant leather ankle-boot descend from the right bank, fall squarely through the middle of my chest, and then move on.

My Emperor's eyes were wide open. In a moment I was on my feet, commanding those boots to return and grovel, but though I raised my voice and shouted, the boots – swooshing beneath Fanny Bertrand's skirt – kept walking. I watched her rustle to the perimeters of the ornamental garden, raise her slender neck, and look up, as if in prayer. She gazed at the sky with her clear indigo eyes and sleeked down her soft shawl, and, although she was but ten yards from me, she had never seemed as distant as she did then. I saw her hand reach out to unlatch the gate and, as I heard the familiar click, it came to me, the thing I had been trying to remember: that last glass of orgeat. A hand guiding it to my lips. "*Drink!*" a voice had murmured, "*that's right . . . bon . . . bon!*" And as I, half-dead, struggled to raise my mouth to the glass, I saw the smile. And there was something wrong in that smile. It was not the kind of smile you offer a dying man. There was something . . . *complacent* in it.

4

I did not follow Fanny through the gate and across the green, but looked back through the deepening blue light, past the pine trees, the half-moon pond and the Chinese pagoda to my old house, inside which, somewhere, must lie the reason for that smile. Just for a moment, there in the east window, I saw Gourgaud standing on a chair, hammering something into the wall. Then a black drape fell between the glass panes and his pale face, and the night sky darkened.

I made no sound on the grass as I walked towards the house framed by black hills and climbed the six steps to the porch. At the top, I passed the small window to the west of the main entrance and, turning my face towards it, was shocked to see that there was no reflection in the glass. I paused for a moment to call for my courage. Then I put my hand to the greasy doorknob, twisted it, pushed and went in.

With what pleasure did I feel the door obeying the thrust of my hand! With what relief! To imagine drifting through the material world like a will-o'-the-wisp, unable to distinguish air from the denser particles of wood; to float, to hover with no homage to substances and boundaries; to feel my hand caving in through the edges of the doorknob as if there was no respect on either side for the principles of matter and space! Such a thing would seem to me – as it did when Fanny Bertrand's foot passed through my chest

- as a world descended into chaos. For even water, the vaguest element, does not occupy the same space as air, and my element had always been earth: fire and earth.

I made a promise to myself then, that I would never allow myself to be passed through again as I had in the ha-ha that night. I refused to be amorphous or ill-defined, to descend into a shifty, fugitive state, drifting through the world like an insubstantial thing. I would go on respecting the orders and borders of old. I would be discrete.

I stood in the gloomy anteroom for some moments, with the wind rushing in behind me, and then I put out a hand and pushed the door to. Several of the candles were guttering on the sideboard, throwing vast shapes against the wall, figures that seemed to flicker and jump to the sighs of Gourgaud who I could hear in the billiard room next door. I had not lived with his browbeating and breast-baring for six years without having learned that sound. At this moment, I guessed, he would be prostrate on the floor, his arms stretched out in homage towards my body, or perhaps kneeling in prayer.

I had no interest in Gourgaud's theatrics, however. It was information that was needed, and I headed straight to my most reliable source: Montholon's diaries.

Everyone, of course, had been writing diaries. Everyone was keeping track. The record-keepers were so many, and their scribbling so frenzied, that sometimes after I had uttered some particularly bon mot, a whole roomful of generals, wives, doctors and servants would excuse themselves and rush out to write it down. One of the few amusements of my exile was to begin - at the very moment we sat down for dinner - a lengthy anecdote that I knew to be of great interest. The courtiers would stop eating, the servants freeze, and across their faces would pass looks of pained constipation as they struggled to store up my words in order to disgorge them correctly later. If I had not known through my own investigations who was writing a diary, I should have guessed it from the frozen expressions of those struggling to remember the exact tenor of what I said. Sometimes, at dinner, I caught glimpses of filled quills beneath napkins, phrases written on the inside of shirtsleeves, or on the arm in ink. Or they would try to remind themselves of my words by forming symbols on their side plates from pellets of bread. "Clear the plates, Pierron," I would say. It amused me, as I have said, in a way.

Of all the accounts being written, Montholon's was infinitely the most superior. How often I had gone to his room to read his diaries when my spirits were low! With what pleasure had I devoured the words and drawings of the man I came to think of as the *most loyal of the loyal,* the man I could always rely upon to produce something fine, something rare. Over the years I had grown tired of the other diaries: Gourgaud's heated passions, Bertrand's pedantic codes, even Marchand's careful recording had begun to annoy me, detailing so laboriously my every mouthful of egg, my every fever and pain. Only Montholon edited out the banal: what I had said about oxen, or the principles of gardening, or roast beef; whether I advised my courtiers to drink claret for breakfast rather than lunch. Only Montholon could properly reproduce my opinions, and set down a satisfactory account of my reflections on war. If I spoke of Pope Pascal or the Battle of Cannæ in the morning, by the evening, in Montholon's diary, the conversation would reappear.

Now, when I opened the door to Montholon's room, I found him sprawled on his narrow bed in the depths of sleep, and even when I closed the door he did not stir.

His eyelids were pulsing and a trail of saliva etched a line from his mouth across his right cheek. As I looked down on him, his lips curled back from his teeth into something between a snarl and a grin.

The room, customarily so tidy, had objects strewn over the floor, and the guard was placed carelessly in front of the fire. The trunk, which usually stood locked behind the door, was open, and, to my irritation, I saw a number of my imperial almanacs and atlases stacked inside. I could not find his green-leather diaries, but at the bottom, beneath a pile of books and a file of well-thumbed pornographic prints, I discovered an unfamiliar black sketchbook, which I lifted out.

You will imagine that a great man is above snooping, but it is not so. A general is only a higher sort of servant and a minion's secrets are, by right, the property of his lord. Indeed, if a man is so reckless as to leave his thoughts lying around, is he not – perhaps hardly knowing it himself – asking to be found out?

So it was that I had many times viewed with a complacent eye such sketches as *The Colossus on his Rock* (me with feet astride the two mountains of this puny island) or *His Majesty Dictating in the Morning*. Montholon flattered me inordinately. Well, I was used to that. And he never sketched me, as he knew I would not have wished, in the loose white pantaloons and colourless shirt that I wore in the mornings. In his sketches I was always majestic, my buttons and shoes always shone, I was three stone slimmer, twenty years younger and my hair always fell in the most imposing of ways.

When I turned to the first page of the sketchbook, you may imagine then the comfort I expected. Myself again: majestic in my bearing, my grandeur, my fame. But the words on the front page brought a taste of fear to my mouth. *Ma Petite Vie, par Napoleon Bonaparte*, had been scrawled there, as if by a child.

The first plate portrayed me, but in it I was distorted even further than in those absurd English cartoons. My belly was doubled, my height halved, and my bicorne hat sat like a silly symbol on my squat head. *Bonaparte Overtaking the Tortoises but Not Much Else*, the caption read, and there I was, pictured in the tiny Longwood garden, striding past a tortoise with a telescope at my eye, and all the paraphernalia of my imprisonment around me: the fences, the cannons, the guards.

The second plate was called *Waterloo the Second*. In it, I stood before a ludicrous papier mâché model, flailing my arms at Gourgaud, who was adjusting the two-inch soldiers on the model according to my command. "We will take it back to the point in the afternoon, before Blucher arrived" I was shown saying from a bubble at my mouth. The expression on my face was ridiculous.

The Emperor Retains His Imperial Grandeur – there I was in my slovenly morning attire covered with coffee stains and cake crumbs. *A Game for Two Giants* – Bertrand and I crouched over a game of tiddlywinks. A cartoon called *Measuring the Children*, with the Bertrands arranged like babushka dolls in a spiralling line of size: Bertrand, Fanny, Hortense, Henri and Arthur. I was the last doll, the solid one, smaller than them all, smaller than their smallest child. *The Emperor Plans His Escape* – sitting at my desk, my head hung in despair. Another: *The Military Genius who Once Controlled the Earth* – there I was doing a jigsaw, putting the pieces of the world in the wrong place. Towards the end: *Bony Plans his Future* – me throwing a noose around a rafter and preparing to hang myself.

The pages went on and on. Whenever I had been ignoble, snarled at the servants or committed an act of uncharacteristic cruelty, he had recorded it. A hundred incidents or more must have been captured by his pen.

I turned the last page of the book and found a letter with the seal of Hudson Lowe, stating that the English censors had approved what they had read:

Paris, 3 Décembre 1820

Cher Marquis Montholon,
  I was fascinated to view the sample sketches of 'the informal moments at Longwood,' and would certainly be interested in publishing them. Whilst it would indeed be possible to circulate them under a pseudonym, as you suggest, I would be negligent not to tell you that should you choose to release them under your own name, and add a small amount of anecdotal text, the price you could command would be very much greater.

*I look forward to discussing the matter with your wife who, I
understand, has left the island and is living again in France. We are
meeting on the 16th of this month.*

Cordialement,
Louis Paton

Behind it, another letter. Unfinished. Unsent. Written that
morning to his wife:

Longwood, 5th May 1821

My Dear Albine,
    *It is all over. He passed away three hours ago, at eleven minutes
to six. We dozed last night in the anteroom, knowing that the end
was near. Every hour or so, one or other of us would go and check
his breathing, or to dab sweetened water between his lips. Each time
we touched him, his cheeks twitched.*
    *This morning, Bertrand, Gourgaud and I stood in a line – like the
soldiers we once were – watching him die. As the sky was leaching
into whiteness, his breathing became stertorous. He coughed a little,
and a speck of blood landed on his white shirt, and for a moment
he opened his eyes and fixed them on my waistcoat. But he saw
nothing, for by then his eyes were dim. A few minutes later, Dr
Antommarchi put a finger to his neck and gave a nod. Bertrand
began sobbing. Then – like the portent the Emperor had long been
waiting for – the dawn gun boomed out from Signal Alarm.*
    *It would be such a comfort to have you here now, my dear. Only
to you could I explain what these six years have meant, and how
things have changed in the two years since you and the child left.
We knew you must leave to escape the emperor's attentions. But still
I have often felt bitter about it.*
    *We must not be parted again when I return. I know you have
been true to me, as I to you, because our fortunes are commingled,
as they have been since our souls first recognised each other, though*

35

mine was reeking of the battlefield. I can never repay fortune for bringing you to me, for allowing you to see what was resting beneath the hoary chest of a soldier.

Perhaps you will get this letter only a few days before I am back. Your last took three months to reach me, and had toured most of the world before it got here. What storytellers letters would be if only they could speak! But darling, it is true. I am, finally, coming home! · I hope I'm not too late. I hope you have not signed anything with Paton. If this letter reaches you in time, please delay making a decision until I am there. If you have already signed, I hope you have not let him cheat you. Tell him, he will have me to answer to if he has.

We must take advantage of recent events. Now his life is over and everything falls into a fixed place: now there are no more possibilities for all the loose ends of his life have been severed like a rope and their ends burnt. With the end, a life falls into a pattern and there is an urge to understand. And if I still know anything about Europe, I guess that she will spend the next five centuries trying to make sense of his life.

I spent one ninth of his life with him, the last, the saddest ninth, and I will always have a place. So do not let Paton undersell you, ma chérie. Be quite –

The letter ended there, as if its author had been disturbed. Hardly aware of what I did, I folded the letter neatly, and put it back as it had been. Then I sat on the bed and looked down on Montholon.

Until that moment, it had never crossed my mind that Montholon, of all people, might betray me. Now, as I looked at him sprawled across the bed, I wondered how long he had been planning it all. A year? Two years? Five? While Bertrand was depressed and Gourgaud throwing jealous fits, Montholon had always been there, dispensing good cheer. I had put it down to his natural disposition, his placid and optimistic spirit. But what if his humour had come, not from sanguinity, as I had always believed, but from his private pleasure in these secret plans and thoughts?

I could hardly believe it – that Montholon should intend to sell satirical drawings of me in France! He knew who would view his cartoons: not my loyal supporters, nor my family, nor the men of the Grande Armée. They would be bought by my bitterest enemies: the Bourbons and the British, those who lived to laugh and see me abased. Did he not know – and he did know! – that caricature, poisoner of reputations everywhere, was deadly in France? I looked down at him with a shiver of dread, because I knew then that I did not know Montholon, despite our common captivity, despite the six years; that I did not know this person with whom I had shared my exile when he left off his public face.

I left the room after some time, and climbed to the attic. I broke my rule and swam through the door so that I should not frighten him, and curled up beside Marchand on the bed. I had an image for a moment, as if floating above myself: my valet and I, like two spoons in a drawer. Then, telling myself there was a long night ahead, I lost consciousness.

5

It is almost midnight. Longwood House is quiet. Napoleon's men have withdrawn, each to poke his own spluttering fire in his own damp room. Baron Gourgaud alone will sit with the dead Emperor tonight.

There has been no thunder this evening, no lightning. These displays of nature rarely occur on St Helena. A small earthquake occurred last year to remind them that there are gods whose favour it is necessary to curry . . . but tonight, nothing of this. The trade winds blow no more fiercely than usual. The atmosphere is still heavy and damp. Just the usual things appear for the man who so believed in signs, for whom the December sun sparkled as he crowned himself Emperor of France. No signs, or portents or atmospheric parallels. Well, isn't that, Gourgaud asks himself, a sign in itself?

The body lies on the green baize billiard table, in the middle of the candlelit chamber, covered to the neck with a white sheet. Although the doors and drapes are closed, Gourgaud can't quite believe himself to be alone either with the body or with Bonaparte. Later he will slip off his clacking shoes, and cushion his ears with the slipping sound of his stockinged feet, but for now formality is still upon him. In this early part of the evening, the public is still peering over his shoulder and stirring the hairs on the back of his neck.

He cannot quite relax. The room has a vivid air: it is the sort of scene that unsettles. He looks down at the Emperor's yellowing complexion; his cheekbones sharpened by illness; his sparse chestnut brown hair, neatly combed. A silver coin – a napoleon – has been placed on each eye, so that bizarrely, each of Bonaparte's sockets also reflects a minted profile of his head. It seems unreal to him that so much has happened in such a short space of time; that he, Baron Gourgaud, can be standing here, looking down . . . on all this . . . .

Gourgaud rubs his eyes and wonders why he offered to sit here tonight. He made the offer instinctively and without thinking: it is an automatic reflex, wanting always to be closer to the Emperor. He is uncertain how to behave; what to do. Nervously, out of old habit, he starts to make up phrases, and, as he does so, the shape of his body changes, becomes tighter and more rigid. His chin and chest rise as he draws himself up and says, extravagantly: "Even in death the Emperor retained his majestic dignity . . . . In death he defied his conquerors, made death itself magnifique."

But in a moment, the proud chin slumps, and the outstretched, declaiming hand reaches up to push aside a strand of hair that is tickling his nose. Gourgaud looks over at the sideboard – at the silver pepper dish with its stomach, and the silver sponge dish containing the heart. "Is it possible to call death magnificent?" he asks himself, passing his fingers through the yellow flames of the candles. Death has the rigour and fixity of magnificence, but he cannot, when he looks at the still body, feel in awe of it. In the night, when the Emperor was dying, Gourgaud had written in his diary:

> We hardly dare touch his body, for it seems to us to possess a
> sort of electric property. Our hands tremble and touch him as if
> he is a sacred object: awe mingled with fear.

39

But in fact here, now, looking down on the body, he feels superior to that motionless cold mass. His own hands are strong and thick-wristed, remind him that he is a man with warm blood still pumping – a drumbeat of survival that goes on – and for this night at least, before the legend of martyrdom is fully spun, he and the Emperor reverse positions. The Baron's hands are brown, mobile, warm. The Emperor's, crossed over the sheet with a white flower wilting between them, are white, fat, dead.

Looking down at the immobile yellow face of Napoleon, Gourgaud feels a sense of superiority, of being one step ahead, and it makes him feel good because the Emperor has not – no, not in any way – treated him as he should.

Gourgaud begins to circle the table as if Bonaparte is his prey. In his laps around the room, he sees not just the ceremony of the present – bees, drapes, candles and order – but, as if painted beneath them, the accessories of the sickroom. The commode was there, at the side of the camp bed with the brown-stained sheets that the Emperor fought against them changing. On the dresser, orgeat, calomel, flannels heating in fire-warmed water. There the blue jar of leeches, and the pots for cupping. And on the bed, the Emperor on one hip or the other, propped into position with a score of white pillows, and blankets over his freezing feet. He wore the vomit-splashed silk robe that he would not let go.

But these things, which for three months and longer have been everything, are now cleared away. No use for medicines now, for draughts and drinks, treatments and potions. After the whims and tantrums and deliriums of the sickroom – the disturbance of a man and his slow passing – the wilful, ailing man is finally snuffed out. It is a relief, thinks Gourgaud, to remember order, to have objects and people in their proper place: oranges in the kitchen, beds in the bedroom, excrement in the commode, and the master at the top of his pyramid, indomitable.

Napoleon had said of Talleyrand: "He is sure to die in his own bed." He meant: *He will die like a woman, not a soldier.* The Emperor had said, "I should have died in Egypt . . . I should have died at Waterloo . . . For history, I should have died at Austerlitz . . . Had the pill not been old, I should have died in Elba . . . ." He had said, "When we are dead, my dear Gourgaud, we are all dead together." But actually they were not.

Gourgaud irritably stretches back the fingers of his left hand and quickens his circuits of the table. He would like to inflict an injury, but is uncertain where to aim. If he were a woman, he might slap the defenceless cold face. If he were a dog, he might sink his teeth into the tempting ankles, gnaw on them like a bone. Instead, he takes out his diary from its usual place beneath his waistcoat and flips through it, catching and slowing the passing of the pages on his long thumbnail. Flicking like this, he can see the ebb and flow of his writing. The many days that are slashed with a single word – *Ennui* – and the others that are packed densely with his tight italicised script.

He reminds himself of his own cause for dissatisfaction. Here it is. April 13th 1816, in words of black ink. He hears, as he reads them, the exact tone in which the dead man said to him:

> *"What right have you to interfere with my affairs? You fancied when you came here that you were to be my comrade, but I am no man's comrade. No-one can reign over me. You expected to be the centre of everything, like the sun among the stars. But it is I who am the sun. If I had known how it would be with you, I would have brought only servants."*

41

His eyes blacken at the black words and he turns to the page of November 18th. It was one of Napoleon's bitterest attacks. A well-thumbed page.

> "Don't bother me with your frankness," the Emperor told me tonight, "Keep it to yourself. Everyone has to dissimulate and learn the art of living with other people. I don't want to hear your opinion of what you call 'my military mistakes', affairs about which you know nothing. What does it matter to me that you are an honest man?"
>
> He dismissed me from the room with a twitch of his wrist, but I was barely out of the door when I heard him saying: "Honestly, Marchand, I truly believe that man is in love with me, and it begins to bore me. I can't take him for my mistress and I don't seem able to send him away. I think it best he seeks his friends amongst the servants and the people of the village from now on."

Gourgaud's fingers are greedy for more evidence and he turns to February 1819.

> This evening, extraordinary events. Marchand rushes in with red cheeks and wild eyes:
> "Sire, they have come to rescue you! A boat is waiting below."
> The Emperor jumps to his feet.
> "They? Who are they? Where is the boat?"
> "I don't know. They have sent a runner and this uniform. Quickly, Sire, there is not much time."
> The light that had sparked in His Majesty's eyes fades. "It is a trick," he tells us.
> "How so?" we cry.
> "Talk to the man," Bertrand exhorts. "Bring him in, Marchand! Vite!"

"And where should I escape to?"

"Majesty –"

"To America? Where no-one knows my name?" The Emperor sits down. "That was never my plan."

Bertrand cries: "You are wrong, Sire. Please! At least bring in the man and hear what he has to say."

"Wrong?" Napoleon jumps to his feet again. "I am WRONG? I was never WRONG at the Tuileries, Bertrand! There I was always right!"

"Sire, s'il vous plaît!" I cry. "S'il vous plaît! Think of your son, of your followers. Think of us!"

"Did I ask you to join me in exile? Do you think I'd have chosen you had I a choice? Job's comforters!" he laughs bitterly. "You only came here to document my decline and fall. Get out!"

He pushes Bertrand and I roughly from the room. Outside the door, I plead again: "Trust me, Sire! Was I not wounded with you at Tabor? Did you not give me your sword at Austerlitz? At Rivoli?"

He slams the door in my face and we hear him shout inside: "Keep that man away from me, Marchand! A parrot could speak more sense than Gourgaud."

Well. The Emperor is silent now. And Gourgaud will speak. The Emperor is silent, and His silence pleases, and with His silence He can return to the glory of former days, become Himself again.

Despite that thought, Gourgaud puts his head in his hands and sighs, for the gamble he took in following the Emperor has been lost, and all his old illusions lie punctured, and draped in dust. When he remembers his high hopes! The duties he performed for the Emperor; his incomparable offices! He takes out his quill, turns to a new page in his diary, and begins to write:

It was I who first entered the Kremlin and blew up the mine that was intended for the Emperor and his Imperial Guard. At Brienne, when the Emperor dropped his sabre, it was I who shot the approaching Cossack. Here, on St Helena, when the grazing cow lifted its tail and turned down its horns to charge, it was me that stepped in front of the Emperor and brandished my sword. I would have saved him again then, had he not taken it upon himself – unnecessarily – to skip nimbly over the wall.

Was I not wounded with him at the Bridge of Tabor? At Austerlitz, did he not give me the sword he had worn at Lodi, Montenotte and Rivoli? For this – for saving his life thrice – how am I repaid? I must pass after Montholon and Bertrand to table, I must have cramped, damp quarters with the smallest of all the generals' fires. I must pace the grounds without conversation, my hand not required for dictation. I am reduced, derided, spat at.

Gourgaud throws down his quill, snaps shut the diary and, with the impatience of a mistress, marches towards the dead man, his tongue weighed down by demands. He realises now that he had expected something to happen at this sitting, as if this, finally, was to be their longed-for tête-à-tête. And again he feels betrayed by the Emperor's stony indifference, his refusal to engage. With his left hand he snatches the sheet from the dead thing before him – clumsily, like a magician who hasn't perfected his act. And with that single wonderful gesture, he understands that the Emperor can no longer shield himself; that Gourgaud may do to his vile body whatever he may wish; that it is he, the Baron, who is victor, finally, tonight.

The stitches along the naked abdomen are neater than Gourgaud remembers. They no longer look like the stitches of a sailor struggling with a rent sail on a stormy night. They look more like the delicate stitches *he* might have made with his embroidery silks when he pretended to listen to Bonaparte reading to them after dinner, in the long evenings.

It is not for love of embroidery that he has plied his needle here, but to cloak his boredom when the Emperor read to them in his expressionless voice, murdering Shakespeare, Ossian and Racine. He needed something in which to bury his eyes because if he looked up . . . if he looked up . . . the Emperor would have seen. So many things that have been destroyed here, so many things that he will never again be able to read! *Antony and Cleopatra* . . . the Emperor's voice quavering as he said, *""What's brave, what's noble, Let's do it after the high Roman fashion, And make death proud to take us,"* and the insinuation was there, filling the room. Gourgaud will never listen to Shakespeare again. He will never again embroider bees.

Gourgaud traces the line of the incision site from the neck, over the bump of the crossed arms to the groin, then slips a nail under one of the loose stitches of the abdomen and pulls his finger up. Although he isn't able to snap the thread, he can force the skin on either side to pucker, and he looks on with disgusted satisfaction as his finger carries out its rhythmic jerk, its *tug, tug, tug.* His eyes move from the belly to the yellowing face where he notices some crusts of gypsum from the afternoon attempt at a death mask. The remnants of the doctors' efforts are smeared around the nose, across the hairline and inside the ears, and Gourgaud resolves to remedy it. He climbs onto the billiard table, allows a large dollop of spittle to fall onto the emperor, then climbs down, takes out his cambric handkerchief, moistens it in the frothy trail, and begins to scour away the whiteness.

Absorbed in his task, Gourgaud does not notice the clock ticking, nor is he aware that he has slipped off his shoes, and is now splaying and relaxing his toes, luxuriating in their freedom on the slippery wooden floor. He will never speak of this moment of intimacy – the naked dead man alone with him. Never once will Gourgaud say: "*I spent a vigorous twenty minutes rubbing away the resid-*

45

ual gypsum from His Imperial Highness's nose." He will never describe to any person the pleasure he gains from being solely in charge, or the joy of such fussing. And, although he knows quite well that tomorrow there will be pomp again – the dressing of the stiff body in clothes no longer needed, the flags and standards and protocols of burial – at this moment, the Emperor is not an emperor to him but a person whom he wants, above all, to torment.

At the thought of his own wounds, Gourgaud scrapes harder and harder at the nose so that tomorrow, for the eye that dares to look Majesty in its dead face, there will be an abrasion in this area, a little worked in grief, a small impression finally, lastingly made. He wants to shake the body awake for this final conversation, to scream in the mucky white ear – *Why did you stop calling me Gorgotto? Why were you afraid to escape?* And to receive a response, a suitable response.

6

Marchand wakes with a start. The Emperor is calling him: "Help me, Marchand, help!"

"Coming, Sire!"

"Now! I need you *now*."

"What do you need, Majesty?"

"Coffee. Then come in here – there's something I want to dictate before the others are up."

Suddenly – as suddenly as it began – the voice disappears and Marchand opens his eyes to find himself lying alone on his bed. He has nursed the Emperor so intently and for so long that he slept last night despite himself. Now, waking, his mind moves very slowly, so that it is his heart which first reminds him that His Majesty is dead, that this morning he must wash him for the final time, dress him for the final time, for the final time shave that beloved face. He strikes a match and looks at his fob: five o'clock. He stumbles from the bed, straightens the jacket he slept in, splashes water over his face, then opens the door of his room straight onto the stairs and the dark outside.

The cicadas are silent now. The mynahs are no longer atwitter. Not even the Longwood strays raise their amorous barks to the moon. This is usually Marchand's favourite time of day: the wind drops in the early morning for an hour or so, the generals are all asleep and – if he is fortunate – the Emperor will call him for dictation, or to hold his razor as he bathes, or to listen as he holds forth on what might have been.

Marchand makes his way to the kitchen, enters, and lights a candle. The embers from last night are still warm in the grate. He throws kindling onto them and waits for the blaze, but he knows in advance that the warmth will not comfort him.

If only he had stood firm. If only he could comfort himself with what had so recently been. If only he could still say that he alone had adhered with integrity to the instructions of the Emperor; that he alone had served him properly and self-effacingly to the end. The man whose orders he has followed for twenty years is gone, the man he has known longer than all the rest. He knows this; he can accept it. He would still have cried if he had done nothing wrong, but the agonising pain comes from knowing he has betrayed the man he has loved for so long.

He never intended to trick him by hiding medicines in his drinks. The Emperor had always known his own mind, and spoken it.

"Marchand," he had said, "you must swear to give me nothing but wine and coffee without my consent. Even when I am weakened beyond speech."

And he had replied: "Majesty, I will not fail to follow any of your instructions."

There had been no cause for misunderstanding. He couldn't comfort himself with that. Looking into the fire before him, he can see the fierce red eyes of the officers and doctors who cajoled him, pulling him away from the death-bed to hiss: "Marchand, the Emperor will die without an evacuation. Is that what you want?"

What could he do with the generals and doctors standing around, menacing him with their eyes, and he the only one that the Emperor would trust? His Majesty had known the trick of course. After the first sip he had turned his tired grey eyes upon him and asked: "What are you hiding in my drinks?"

"They say you will die without calomel, Majesty," he had sobbed, "that you must on all accounts pass a stool."

The Emperor had closed his eyes wearily and said: "You swore my wishes were sacred to you," and in that moment Marchand felt he would have given his life to reverse what he had done.

Bertrand had come later to comfort him. "What love there was in the Emperor's reproach! You did what was best."

But Marchand cannot forgive himself, or them.

"It is dishonourable," he had told Bertrand, "not to respect the wishes of a dying man. We think that because we still possess our full minds, we know what is right, what is best."

"That's enough," Bertrand had said. "That's enough."

Marchand is fully awake now, and the fire is blazing. Whilst he waits for the water to boil, he begins to lay a tray, and, since Baron Gourgaud was not one of the ones who cajoled, Marchand sets out for him the last un-chipped cup from the Imperial China. Of course they had all been desperate, of course they had all wished that it might not be so; hoped beyond anything that the Emperor's life might be saved. But duplicity was not the way. The Baron had, after all, behaved as a good man. He had cared for the Emperor. Despite the odd things he said, he had cared for him – in his strange, unnatural way.

He knocks on the billiard room and enters quietly.

"Good morning, monsieur. I trust you passed a tolerable night."

"Marchand!" Gourgaud wakes with a start and rubs his eyes. "What time is it?"

"Just after five. I've brought you some coffee."

Gourgaud looks up, and follows Marchand's eyes to the naked Emperor. It is not, in his waking state, a pretty sight. He stands up with a guilty look and watches as Marchand covers the cadaver.

"I have just awoken, sir. I apologise for not coming sooner. Was it windy in the night?" he says gesturing to the sheet. "Is . . . every-thing well with you?"

"Quite well." Then reluctantly: "And with you?"

"As it can be."

Gourgaud walks towards the billiard table and looks down. He watches Marchand fiddle with the cover for a moment, adjusting the angle of the sheet, smoothing out the wrinkles. Then he says: "The body must be guarded until it is buried. I told Bertrand that. There are men out there," he waves airily in the direction of the English camp, "who would rip his body open to steal their pound of flesh. You look shocked, Marchand. Don't you think it's possible?"

"I hope not, monsieur."

"Believe me, it is." He pulls the tassel of the bell on the wall beside him, and they hear it ring in the kitchen.

"Even among our own court, there are some who, well . . . might like a souvenir of flesh. Who do you think most likely? Bertrand? Ummm . . . too fastidious? Probably. Montholon? The man's a dark horse; couldn't bet on what he'd do. No . . . above all, I think Fanny is the one most likely to execute a daring raid: a finger, per-haps? Half a foot? Or something frighteningly internal. An eye? A tooth? The very fact that we can consider it means it is possible."

He rings the bell again, and its clamour echoes through the house.

"There is no-one to answer, sir."

"I know."

Gourgaud moves over to adjust a drape that is letting in a chink of night. Then he turns towards Marchand and says: "Everyone is happy for me to do the sitting. They know that body snatching is not my thing."

"Of course not, sir. Of course not." Marchand's face puckers with distaste.

Marchand remembers the way that the French fought for the largest piece of autopsy sheet; the way that the English sheared off locks of hair, and Antommarchi carved himself a piece of imperial rib. He wants to say: "Of course, no one will commit such sacrilege," but actually today he is no longer sure.

Marchand looks down at the Emperor's beloved face, and wonders how so much can change in such a short space of time. It seems unreal to him that he and Baron Gourgaud can really be conversing like this. He turns his face towards Gourgaud and says quietly: "He must be sat with out of respect, sir, because these are his first hours as a dead man."

Gourgaud's fingers move to pull the bell again and then stop.

"I have never laid out a body before, Marchand, have you?"

"Oui, monsieur. I will show you what to do. We must shave the head too, for the death mask, as you know, and because the emperor asked for hair bracelets to be sent to his family. Give me a minute to get the water."

Marchand is desperate to wash the Emperor, to erase from his body every last trace of mucus and blood, to make him holy again and clean, despite the stitches, despite the abdomen only half-filled with organs and packed, like a scarecrow, with straw.

He is sure he will never get over the shock of the autopsy – to see that organs can be sliced with as little effort as roast beef. It is still shocking to him that Napoleon's organs should have been seen! "Now the stomach," Chapman had commanded, as if the Emperor's stomach should remove itself from its abdominal seat and present itself curtsying before him. That sacred interior! Exposed to the vulgar eye! That every organ should be pronounced just 'healthy' or 'diseased' as if Majesty cannot be seen – aye! – even in the very tubes of one's bladder, and the curves of one's spleen. And then to see the dissected organs discarded, and the body stuffed with straw. "Will you not reunite all the entrails with the body?" he had asked, and the surgeon had said, "Well, I don't think he has much need for them anymore, Marchand, do you?"

Marchand pushes these thoughts aside, and leaves the room with vigour in his step. He is rejuvenated suddenly by knowing that there are still duties left to perform. He brings back the water, crosses himself, and pours the remains of the Emperor's cologne into the bowl. He moves to the end of the table, and uncovers the right leg. He soaks a flannel in water and starts to wash, beginning at the thigh, and moving over the bulge of the knee, along the thin skin of the shin, around the ankle and the toes to the yellowing sole of the foot. When he has completed the circular movements with the napkin he takes a dry cloth and repeats the pattern, thigh to foot.

"If you hold up the leg, sir, I can wash underneath."

"Of course," says Gourgaud moving round, and lifting the limb. "Would it not be easier to take off the shroud?"

"Easier, sir, but not so respectful, I think."

"And is it always for you to tell us what is right, Marchand? Is that what you think?"

Silence hangs in the air. Marchand does not know how to answer. He would like to beg to be alone for this final washing; to explain that, although he is a servant, there are intimate things he wishes to say confidentially to the dead body of his friend. He wants to shout: "I too can be trusted; I too can feel and understand!" But instead he shakes his head to oust the thought and says: "I apologise, sir. I did not mean to cause offence. I meant only that though it would be easier, sir, it is not what is usually done."

"Alright, Marchand, get on with it!" Gourgaud picks up the opposite leg. "It's not for pleasure that I break my back with this weight."

"It *is* easier if the corpse is fresh. But once *rigor mortis* has set in . . . ."

"We should have done it earlier then."

Marchand doesn't wish to tell him that this too is a matter of respect.

Marchand cleans swiftly and effectively, eradicating the effluence of life and the autopsy, but all the time wishing that instead of speed there might be reverence! Instead of duty, love! How he wishes that he could say what he thinks.

He removes the silver coins from the eyes, and the strip of cloth intended to bind the mouth shut.

"Now, sir, we can roll him and wash his back. I'll count to three. On the third count we'll pull him towards us. Very well. Un . . . deux . . . trois. Not too hard, Baron, otherwise he'll be right over! C'est vrai! Just there! Do you have him? Bien. Just a moment."

Marchand runs around the table and wets his towel in the bowl.

"Are you comfortable, sir?"

"It's damned heavy. Just stop talking and hurry up."

Gourgaud, stooping to hug the body towards him, finds his face just inches from the Emperor's, and his belly, when he thinks about it, is pressing at this very moment into his. When he looks down, he can see, within the Emperor's slightly open jaw, his swollen gums and coffee-stained teeth. The sight unnerves him and he turns his gaze away, peering over Napoleon's back to follow the circular movements of his valet's cloth.

"All done, sir. Just give me a moment, and I'll help you roll him back down."

But Gourgaud is impatient and thinks he can do it alone, and only when the body has over-balanced does he realise that he hasn't got the strength to stop it crashing down. The head and neck jerk rigidly up and down as they land, and the crossed arms flap up and down. When he looks at the head he sees to his horror that one of the eyelids has flung itself open, and the creamy viscous jelly of the eyeball stares back at him, monstrous without its iris.

Marchand hurries to the other side, places a finger over the eyelid and smoothes it back down.

53

Neither of them speaks. Gourgaud does not apologise nor Marchand accuse. The skin is grazed across the elbow, where the body fell against a silver brush, but there is, of course, no blood.

Marchand coughs, rubs the elbow – as if soothing a child's knee – and tries not to weep. He reminds himself of the importance of remaining impassive. He reminds himself of the tasks ahead: still the arms, chest, neck and head to wash. He takes another cloth and soaks it in scent. He would like to press the damp rag to his forehead, his face, to soak himself forever in that smell: orange blossom and lemon. He squeezes the wet rag in his palm and feels the cologne drip between his fingers.

"Marchand!" Gourgaud points at the drip.

Impossible to explain to this man, that aroma is what he seeks.

The Emperor's body is so familiar to him that even without looking he knows the scar on the head, the one on the left ring finger, the deep hole in the arm, the cautery wound on the thigh.

He takes a breath and pulls the sheet up so that it covers just the legs. His cloth goes smoothly around the Emperor's groin, his testicles, his penis, and then a different cloth follows, to dry. The size of his testicles, their hairlessness, are not a surprise to the man who has bathed him for twenty years. He knows every part of his body – is loving it – even as Gourgaud looks away.

As the servant's hands move below him, Gourgaud looks down at the wound on the Emperor's arm. He does not want to ask, but, unable to help himself, he points to the old scar: "What was that from, Marchand?"

"From Austerlitz."

Gourgaud pauses. His voice is odd as he says: "I did not know that the Emperor was wounded there."

"No, His Majesty always tried to keep his wounds secret. He said that people would think he was indestructible, even divine, if he survived so much conflict uninjured."

Gourgaud's mouth and lips purse together into a clean white line. Why had he not known that? Why should the Emperor confide in a servant, but not in him?

The silence carries for a long time. At last Gourgaud says: "You see my finger, Marchand?"

"Oui, monsieur?"

"The lump. It's a fine lump, is it not?"

"It is rather raised."

"That, as I told Montholon last evening, is what comes from holding a quill all these hours. From His Majesty's dictation."

Marchand does not reply.

"Have you seen Bertrand's fingers?"

"I believe so, sir, but they have not caught my particular attention."

"Montholon's?"

"Again, sir, I have not noticed anything remarkable."

Gourgaud seizes Marchand's hand and prizes it away from the cadaver.

"Well, look at your own, then."

He holds his own finger alongside Marchand's, comparing lumps.

"Do you see that yours is much larger," he says unpleasantly.

"I must say, sir, I have barely noticed it with everything that has been going on." Marchand shakes his finger loose and pulls away.

"What did the Emperor dictate to you, Marchand?"

"Oh many things, sir. The codicils to his will, as you know. But before he was ill, the battle of Jena mainly. And Russia."

"That doesn't surprise me. Bertrand had Egypt; Montholon had Elba and Waterloo. Do you know what I had?" He pauses dramatically. "I had Italy, Marchand!"

Marchand is dabbing the face dry. "You were not pleased with Italy, Baron?"

"Italy!" Gourgaud scoffs. "The early campaigns? Victories undoubtedly, but simple victories, a mere foothill to the mountain that was to come. Napoleon Buonaparte was just a soldier then, a lucky, clever soldier. But he was not an emperor, or a god, or a beast. He had not become . . . *sublime*."

"But it was the beginning of everything, sir. Le début. It was an honour, was it not, to have the Emperor share his recollections with you? If you would just lift the arm now, Baron, as you did with the leg."

"I suppose it is different for me, Marchand. You should be honoured. You were his valet. But I am a Baron."

"That is true sir, but still . . . for one such as the Emperor . . . ."

"*He* needed *us*, Marchand! How else could he circulate his ideas when he was forbidden to publish in Europe under his own name? Without our help, Napoleon would not be a legend: he would be just one more exile, dying in a lonely place, forgotten in time."

Marchand takes up a brush and begins to lather the darkly-peppered jaw. He shaves quickly, knowing as he does every contour and plane of the familiar face. Then he cleans and sharpens the razor, and begins to soap the scalp.

"It has been my honour to serve him."

"For me, you must see, Marchand, it is different."

Marchand pauses to wipe the sweat from his brow and says: "I am sure that the Emperor did not intend to slight you, sir, at any point."

"Ah well Marchand, you would think that. You have heard the saying that no man is a hero to his valet."

"Oui."

"Well you are the living refutation of that."

"The Emperor was a colossus to me. He always treated me as a friend."

"That is my point, Marchand. You, who could expect so little, received so much."

After another long pause, Gourgaud asks: "Do you have no regrets, Marchand? No regrets at all?"

Marchand looks up in surprise. An egalitarian question from the man for whom hierarchy has meant so much. Gourgaud is looking at him, honestly interested for one short moment in Marchand as a man.

"I regret that we doctored the Emperor's drinks," he says at last, running the sharpened razor between his fingers. "And everything else we have done to interfere."

7

For three days I hung around the house in a pitiful state. As each fresh betrayal was revealed, a small part of me died. There was so much I hadn't known; so much I hadn't seen.

I hid myself around the house and grounds of Longwood House as a child might its mother's skirts. It was comforting to me – I'm no longer ashamed to admit it – to hear the voices of my old companions around me: as long as I could hear Bertrand's dull intoning voice, or Pierron's squabbles with Marchand in the kitchen, or young Arthur squealing with joy over blind man's buff, I could pretend that all was not lost. Had they not called me Emperor? Bowed and quivered before me? "I am in the next room," I told myself. "I can summon them before me, if I choose."

At certain times I was able to maintain such thoughts. At others, the conversations in the house – about my funeral outfit, or the four coffins in which I was to be buried (tin stacked inside oak, inside lead, inside mahogany) brought me to what was left of my senses.

Not once in those three days did it occur to me to leave Longwood. It seemed impossible to leave the house and garden that I had long raged against, because to leave them would be to acknowledge the change in my condition. And, in the many years that I had dreamt of this moment of release, I had never once envisaged creeping away along an empty road without a single pair of eyes following me. For years and years and years, as long as I could remember, I had carried myself – even in privacy, even in the bedroom, or the tent – as if eyes might at any time be upon me, and I found that I had no idea how to walk now that no-one watched my progress. The land outside Longwood terrified me: I did not know what horrors lay beyond the sentry post, the grassy hill, the isthmus. I had spent six years within the windswept acre of my exiled village and, without being aware of it, I had shrunk to fit its size.

On the third day of this inconclusive state, a conversation took place that tore me from my twilight state of nostalgia and excuses, and propelled me forward on the relentless march of destiny.

The Governor's aide-de-camp, Gorrequer, had arrived with a copy of the autopsy report, which he was insisting Antommarchi should sign.

He explained the situation to Montholon: "All the English surgeons have signed. Only Antommarchi still refuses. He told me: *'I cannot in good conscience sign a report from which my comments on the enlarged liver have been expunged.'* The Governor is furious. He has already spoken to the English officers and told them that any *mention* of an enlarged liver is a court martial offence. I really think it best that Antommarchi does sign. I can't answer for what will happen if he does not."

Montholon looked thoughtful for a moment, then nodded and said: "Leave it to me, Gorrequer."

"You're all coming to Plantation House for the dinner prior to the reading of the will?" Gorrequer asked.

"Yes."

"Shall the Governor send the carriages for you at five?"

"Merci."

"And the burial should be arranged for tomorrow afternoon?"

"That will give us time."

Gorrequer saluted and left.

Montholon sat back in his chair for some time deep in thought. I watched him sitting motionless in the shade of the blue-gum trees, with fairy-terns wheeling in the branches above him and bees buzzing thickly through the air. At last, he rang the bell and asked for Antommarchi, and, when the doctor arrived, Montholon looked at him silently for some moments. When he could see Antommarchi was uncomfortable, he said: "Mon cher Francesco, is it really worth it?"

He paused and fixed the doctor with a condescending smile. "The truth is Napoleon died of cancer, and everything else is just quibbles. If you will forgive me saying so bluntly, quibbles have been the source of your trouble here, and one of the reasons the Emperor was so displeased with you."

"What do you mean?"

"Was it politic to say when you first met him: 'It will be interesting to treat a live patient. Until now, I have had only corpses.' Was that a tactful thing to say?"

"I meant it as a joke."

"One should be certain of one's audience before one sets oneself up as a wit. In such a way have jesters and fools been beheaded by kings."

"I did not come here to receive lessons."

"But it is not for want of needing them."

Antommarchi looked down, and his face assumed that implacably sullen look I knew so well.

"Francesco," Montholon said soothingly, pouring him a glass of Madeira, "you are a young man. Take the advice of an elder who intends you well."

"I would have thought, Marquis Montholon, that you, at least, would have respect for the truth."

"But we have the truth," Montholon said with exasperation.

"The Emperor asked me to make an exact and detailed report of his post-mortem. '*Neglect nothing,*' he told me, '*so that when you see my son you can explain everything to him.*' No, Marquis Montholon!" Antommarchi held up a hand. "Let me go on."

"I trained with the great Mascagni of Florence and was chosen to come here by the Emperor's own mother. While I may have inadequacies as a physician, as an anatomist I have no rival on this island. On the matter of the autopsy, if nothing else, I think my opinion should be noted."

Montholon looked around irritably and coughed. Antommarchi went on: "Everyone knows that French and Italian medicine is superior to English. What do the English know about science? Cancer is not the only possible explanation for the eroded pylorus, you know. In my time, I've seen them caused by diet, by anxiety, by swallowed bile, even by fools who have drunk household poisons. Similarly, climate is not the only possible cause of an enlarged liver. The liver, Marquis, is the processor of the body's toxins. Any substances that the body considers poisonous – "

"Do you know that in an earlier copy of his will the Emperor left you a legacy?"

Antommarchi's face brightened. "Really?"

"Yes. He wrote: '*I leave Antommarchi nine francs to buy a rope to hang himself.*' Those were his words."

Montholon continued smoothly, "If the Emperor's true opinion of you were to become known, your career would be ruined in Europe."

"What do you mean?"

Montholon took a sip of wine and then carefully laid out a saucer of water for the bees.

"Think of it this way. Only a small group of people know that he called you a charlatan and a fool. Remember how he laughed at you for espousing the beliefs of Gall and Lavater? Remember how he said it was ridiculous to believe that a soul could be read in a face? You know how he destroyed the Governor's reputation? So might he easily have done yours."

"I have done nothing like Sir Hudson Lowe."

"I do not wish to brag, or make you feel indebted to me, but it was me who insisted that the Emperor burn that old will and its dreadful insult."

"Was it?" Antommarchi asked dully.

"Yes. I told His Majesty: *'This is a young man with his professional life ahead of him. Forgive his ignorance, his foolishness,'* and he did. I shall be most irritated if you now willingly destroy your own future yourself."

Antommarchi looked at him curiously, but did not interrupt.

"You keep saying that the liver was enlarged, but no-one else it found so. Don't you think you might have imagined it, because you heard the Emperor say so often that this would be the case?"

Antommarchi shook his head decidedly. Montholon sighed.

"If you do not sign, the English will destroy you: they will disseminate the Emperor's opinion of your professional skill. Are you going to ruin yourself for the man who abhorred you, who would have ruined you without a thought, with just a motion of the pen? The Emperor had no respect for doctors. Why then should you respect him?"

"But the English don't know the Emperor's opinion of me."

Montholon looked intently into Antommarchi's face: "He's dead. It's all over. What's the point of quibbling? You have done well."

"You think then that I should sign?"

There was a long pause. Then Montholon nodded.

"I shall have to reconsider. If I do sign, I will draw up a private report of my own findings."

Montholon smiled. "You must do what your conscience dictates; whatever you think is right."

That conversation was the sounding brass in my head, the final proof that I was still required to act. I had been drifting around aimlessly, as if I were no more than a spectator to these events. Now I realised that the final chapter of my book had still to be written, and that without that chapter, nothing that had gone before would make sense. Without it, all the suffering I had chosen to sow for myself would yield nothing.

For the first time, I began to consider whether the findings of the autopsy were correct. I had – in my secret heart – believed I was dying of stomach cancer and had listened complacently as the doctors concluded just that. But had my own assumptions warped my understanding? Had my impatience and irritation with the idiot Antommarchi led me to listen imperfectly? How I wished I could reverse time and have another look.

When I had shouted that the English were killing me, I had meant by climate, by isolation and a thousand pinpricks of maltreatment, "bled to death by paper cuts," as I once put it to Marchand. Now, I began to consider whether the English had really been the authors of a more nefarious plan, for why otherwise should they care so much what Antommarchi said about my liver?

I had to go to Plantation House: that much was clear. I could no longer fool myself that things would develop as I had foreseen. My son's future depended upon some final touches: the public declaration of my will; the proper conclusion of my plan.

I had not seen my body for three days, since the afternoon of the autopsy, but now I went inside to pay it a visit.

It was disturbing to see my old flesh, encased in ice, lying in a darkened chamber. The gloom was relieved only by ten candles, burning in a candelabra shaped like a pyramid. Seeing it, I thought again that I should have stayed in Egypt: had I remained there, I should have become Emperor of the entire orient by now, greater even than Alexander.

Once I had owned the earth, and everything upon it was covered with my emblems, with eagles and bees, and the whole of Paris was carved with N next to N. Now the black cloths that hung at the windows - embroidered in gold with the Bonaparte bees - were one of the few material remains of my empire. I remembered asking Bertrand to pack them when I was gathering my things around me at Malmaison. Although the English were baying like hounds for me outside, I remember the cool manner in which I had packed books, clothes and maps. Most of these items the enemy had not allowed me to bring, but these death drapes were one of the few things they let me keep.

Perhaps my emotional state was heightened at that time, or perhaps it was the strange light cast by the candles, but the gold bees on the curtains seemed to glow brighter than usual. In my disturbed state, they seemed to come alive again, to buzz imperially around my body, as if animated for one final duty.

"Bonjour, Marchand," I said, but my old valet, who was sleeping in a chair beside my body, did not respond. I tried to wake him - to confirm something I had begun to suspect - that my physical powers were diminishing. Three days ago I had been able to open doors and move objects with little more effort than when I was alive. Now it was only with enormous concentration that I could make contact with the material world. As I tried now to shake Marchand, my hands kept slipping through the contours of his body, and it was only with the greatest effort that I was able to pinch the lobe of his ear. He stirred as I did this, but did not wake.

It was clear that my physical abilities were diminishing, and that perhaps I had little time, yet that knowledge changed nothing: despite repeated attempts at the sideboard, I was unable to pick up and examine my pickled stomach. I shifted back to the main body, thought about pressing my lips to my own dead head, but could not bring myself to do it. Instead, I saluted myself, and left.

Standing outside in the damp wind with the smell of my stomach on my hands, I examined the scene before me. There to the north was the English camp. Flashes of their red uniforms and glints from their stacked bayonets carried across the distance, and smoke rose from their many fires. There was festivity in the air. Banjos and mouth organs and the deep bass of men's singing broke the stillness from time to time, and the aroma of curry came to me on the air. The points of the canvas bivouacs and the curves of the turtle-shell roofs that had broken my skyline for six years were disappearing. Everything was changing. Everyone was packing up to leave.

My courtiers were standing in the garden watching the carriages approach. When the first of the two carriages stopped, I went ahead of Gourgaud and Montholon and climbed in.

I watched them on that journey the entire time; watched them more closely than I had done for years, perhaps ever. And I thought: *How is it that I have never come to know these men?*

At first, they appeared to be sitting companionably together, in an untroubled sort of silence. The coachman's whip seemed not to worry them, nor the rattling of the coach. After some time Gourgaud stretched his arms above him and let out a luxurious yawn.

Suddenly he laughed and said: "I feel like a child, knowing that the long vacation is approaching. The whole world is opening up."

Montholon turned and looked at him. "Yes, I know what you mean."

The two men had spent the exiled years bickering. Now, in my death, they appeared to have become friends.

"What will you do?"

"Return to Albine. To the children," Montholon said, and his voice was the closest I had ever heard it to wistfulness. "And you?"

"To my mother, of course." Gourgaud laughed shyly. He went on: "It is not as the Emperor said. Do you remember him telling me that I would never see her again? But it is he that is dead, not she."

He paused and let out a satisfied sigh. "I would never have said that to you in our exile. I think prison must annihilate one's desire to tell, and to know. Only in freedom can one wish to know the woes and delights of other men."

Montholon looked at him in surprise, then nodded. "Perhaps you are right."

Gourgaud put out a hand and clasped Montholon's shoulder, then shifted his long body and let out another luxurious yawn. "These endless wakes are tiring me. I must rest tonight while some-one else sits. It is a pleasure that I am still getting used to, you know, to sit when I want and to retire when I am tired. Do you remember how he made us stand in his presence while he sat? For hours, and hours, and hours!"

Montholon nodded.

Then, when the carriage had turned a bend in the road, Gour-gaud turned and, giggling like a child, cried: "Unbelievable, Mon-tholon! We shall leave in less than a week for *Europe!*" and he raised his head and shouted through the window: "*To Europe!*" And the echo went on long after we had passed through that bare valley.

These men were the sacred custodians of my name, yet they seemed to have no idea that what they said in the weeks ahead would have more effect upon my reputation than anything they could have said when I was alive! Only these men could make my legend endure. Shouting "*To Europe!*" in the quiet of the afternoon for the ears of island dwellers and English soldiers. "*À l'Europe!*" How I hated them at that moment.

I turned and looked at Montholon. A wry smile was on his face. He looked as if he'd just snatched a girl secretly from her long-term lover, and that his rival did not know it. At that moment I would have given anything to know what he was thinking, I who had never spent a minute considering the inner life of my men.

Gourgaud I had understood. He was half in love with me, of course, and treated me as though I was his mistress, as if every word of favour I bestowed on someone else was an insult to him.

But Montholon I had never known. He had treated me well, that is all I could say, except at the end, when he thought my mind was elsewhere. But who he truly was, the man I had not known before St Helena, who had links to the king and the old crown, I could not now say. The things he smiled at and the impulses of his heart seemed, at that time, to be mysteries that I should never learn. It was only one of the ways in which I was wrong.

Occupied by such thoughts, I barely noticed at first what was passing outside the carriage. As we rumbled on, the path wound round and round, snaking back on itself, twisting, turning, so that in a short time I could no longer point out the direction of Longwood. When the road passed near to the coast, the land was arid with boulders and brown-orange beds of lava twisted and deformed into nightmarish shapes. When the road turned inland, it was green and lush and I saw mangoes, lemons and bananas. The peaks themselves were wet and tropical and covered with vast palm-like ferns that looked as though they belonged to a time when monsters roamed the earth.

I had passed well beyond the boundary of my former prison and now I knew what lay beyond it: what lay along the paths I had passed through only once on my way to Longwood six years ago, when the lethargy of imprisonment was upon me and a screen of despair hemmed in my sight. I had fooled myself over the years that all of St Helena was like Longwood – rain and storms and winds howling around our ears day and night. Now I saw that the whole continent of Europe, in miniature, was here. For the island, though tiny, had such various landscapes – swamp, volcano, grassland, mountain, arid cliff, forest, garden – that it seemed vastly bigger than its ten miles by six. Such variety of life thrived here that I wondered how it was that *I* had not thrived, and I wondered what would have happened had I been put in the dry heat, or in the grasslands, or in the orchards in the centre of the island. What if I had lived amongst rice fields or could have walked in the afternoon sunlight through fields of cows and seen their udders filling with life-giving milk?

The richness of the island assaulted me – the smell of citrus, a white bird in flight, the dark wormy life of the soil – and when I contrasted that with my little house in the coldest, wettest corner of the island, and the few pokey wooden rooms that had enclosed me, I wanted to weep. Then I thought of Lowe and the British and my son, and I knew that if all my suffering were to mean something, as I had always intended it should, there was a great deal more for me to do.

8

I ask myself now: what did I expect to find at Plantation House? Instructions from the Governor to his chosen assassin? Written proof of his murderous intent? Letters colluding in bizarre plots? I do not know exactly. It just seemed imperative at the time that I should be there to hear the reading of my will and also to see . . . what? Dropped clues? Hidden evidence? Signs that only I could interpret and see? The truth is, I can no longer remember. I can only remember what I found, and that, pulling into that driveway, I was stabbed by a dagger of jealousy stronger than anything I had felt for years. They had told me there was no house on the island fit for an emperor. Yet here it was: vast, classical, and golden in the late afternoon light, with lawns stretching smooth for hectares, sloping towards a cliff overlooking the sea. Here the wind did not blow. A forest protected the house, and the weather was balmy. The garden was full of plants that suggested warmth and occasional, gentle rain.

As we drew up to the grand entrance and my courtiers climbed down, I watched their faces. I hated them then: hated them for having life beyond me, hated them for having decided to come. It was the first invitation they had had in years, and they had jumped at the chance. I should have known that the minute my back was turned, they would be out basking like lizards in the sun.

I could sense the excitement that lay beneath their mock solemnity, how thrilled they were to be meeting properly the English jailor I had forbidden them to see. The Governor seemed determined to put himself out, speaking French, anxious to show respect to the people whose lives he had, by chance, been sent to police.

"Enchanté," I heard Bertrand say, and watched with disgust as he leaned forward to kiss an English-woman's hand.

"If it pleases you, we shall have supper before we retire next door," Lowe said in stumbling French. More kisses, more Enchantés.

Bertrand smiled and said in a hideously ingratiating manner: "Merci, Sir Hudson. We appreciate your attentions."

As they stood uttering nonsensical pleasantries, switching from French to English and back again, the eyes of my courtiers wandered everywhere: to the velvet chaises longues, the polished silver, the royal portraits on the walls. They gazed at everything with the wonder of savages, or, like paupers taken for the first time to a grand house, as if they had never seen my palaces or the far finer things I had owned. Fanny Bertrand's fascination was obscene, but then women are nothing but barbarians at heart. I should have persuaded the French to lock them in harems, as the Arabs do, when I had the chance.

They sat on the cool, stone terrace, with Chinese servants moving silently among them, and the distant sea glinting in the moonlight. The Governor and Lady Lowe sat at opposite ends of the long table separated by an abundance of crystal, candles and gleaming silver.

I must confess that my ghostly mouth seemed to salivate as the dishes arrived: quails eggs with sweet peppers and roe; wild peacocks braised with peach; and a dolphin that came whole, flambéed in brandy and blazing blue to the table.

"This fellow dropped in this morning," Lady Lowe said indicating a huge sea-turtle, which lay belly up, its abdomen filled with a creamy broth. "They don't often turn up at St Helena, especially grand old boys like this – he must be from Ascension Island, or even Africa. I believe he weighed in at over two hundred pounds. Countess Bertrand, may I offer you some?"

"I should like to pay homage to the creature who has made such a long swim."

"Seven hundred miles from Ascension Island," Lowe remarked.

"And that is the nearest spot of land to here?"

"Yes," said Lady Lowe gesturing to a servant to fill Fanny's bowl. She raised her eyes comically to the sky and said: "How did this tiny spit of land ever come to be here? The Americas on one side, and Africa on the other, with the great moat of the Atlantic in-between! It seems against all common sense that this little rock should be here." She paused and took a sip of wine and then looked mischievously at her husband and then at Montholon. "They say that the devil spat it on his way between the two continents."

"The island is a volcano," Bertrand said gravely, "a mountain whose shoulders protrude above the waters of the ocean, as we see in Corsica and Elba. It has simply not erupted for many years, just as Vesuvius has only rumbled since Pliny's time."

Lady Lowe smiled and said: "I believe what you say, Count Bertrand. But to me the question is more interesting if you think of it this way: Why should God have ordained that on this little spot a dwelling place for man and beast should be?"

"St Helena was not ordained, Madame. It is merely one of nature's phenomena."

Lady Lowe smiled again and turned to the other men. "I prefer my explanation to yours, Count Bertrand. I think it has been conjured up by the fevered imaginations of men. The seafarers thought they had discovered paradise when they first saw it."

"How different to our own experience," Gourgaud said dryly. "It looked more like hell."

"But to come across it in the middle of a long sea voyage, Baron Gourgaud! When it has been weeks and weeks since you have smelt land, or seen anything but the endless grey waves! To see lemons and oranges and fresh water and waterfalls, and meat on the shore, goats, and fowls! Under such circumstance you must admit, it would seem like heaven."

"I have no image of heaven, Madame," Gourgaud said petulantly. "It would be pleasant to eat meat again, certainly, and to set foot on earth that did not move. Under such circumstances did we come to Longwood, and the land looked pleasant enough after so long at sea. But we saw the reality soon enough."

"Of course," Lady Lowe said quickly, looking at her husband. "Illusions usually pass." She took a short sip of wine and waved for the servants to start serving the dolphin.

A donkey brayed in the distance, insistently. "Did you know," said Lady Lowe, laughing, "that they call the donkeys the nightingales of St Helena? Delightful, isn't it?"

For two hours they chewed like cattle, whilst I looked on with fury. I had never been able to bear these bovine habits at table, this slow eating and drinking that ate away the hours. I fed like a soldier even when a civilian, even when I was an exile and had hours and hours and hours. Now I was repulsed by their bestial greed: by Bertrand's noisy chewing, by the spittle around Gourgaud's mouth, by Montholon's stomach rumbling at the unaccustomed delights.

How did these pathetic men still exist - drifting and floundering through life in the ridiculous way of common men - whilst I, the genius of living, was fading from it . . . becoming spectral. Only I knew what to do with life; only I had opened my mouth and crunched into it all: meat, fat, tendon, gristle, marrow, bone. How had the gods allowed it? How could they bear to see me go...?

I was dead, and I had never been so angry about anything else in my life. Not at Talleyrand's betrayal, at Joséphine's inability to bear me children, at my mother for sleeping with other men. The dead are always portrayed as cross-legged and serene, painted reclining on couches, talking wisdom and philosophy. But this was not death for me. All I had were the shoddy tools of the ghostly life, which I utilised now with fury - blowing air up Fanny Bertrand's skirts, knocking peas from Montholon's fork, putting a spectral finger to Bertrand's wine and tipping it across the table. As the liquid splashed across the table, they all screeched like women and then laughed.

"Je suis désolé," said Bertrand, aghast, "I don't know what happened. I hardly seemed to touch the glass."

"Perhaps the ghosts are thirsty," said Lady Lowe, laughing and signalling for the spillage to be cleared up. "I told you we have them here. They do the strangest things. Sometimes at night before Hudson and I retire, we hear one of them - we think he must be an old caretaker - closing the windows and shutters all round the house. He starts in the east wing and moves to the west in a rather orderly fashion. But he never closes the windows in the room in which one is."

"And do you hear this too, Sir Hudson?" Montholon asked sceptically.

Lowe laughed. "I am not so fancifully inclined as my wife."

"Hudson, you know it is true! You've heard it."

"Perhaps I have, my dear, but I choose not to believe."

Fanny Bertrand looked at Lady Lowe. She seemed to hesitate before she said: "My mother swore that there was a ghost of a child in our house in Orléans, and she could hear her crying sometimes at night."

Gourgaud looked at her with contempt. "Does it not strike you that it is always women who hear such things?"

"Perhaps because women are more sensitive," Lady Lowe retorted.

"But what would one do if one wanted to get rid of this ghost?" Montholon asked, archly. "What if next week you're tired of him, or fed up with him disturbing your evenings?"

"I don't believe you can do anything. Ghosts exist as entities distinct from us. We might occupy the same space, but we cannot communicate."

"But is he not communicating with you when he closes the windows?"

"I don't believe so. It is just his old habit."

"You seem very sure of things, Lady Lowe."

"I am. So would you be, after so many years in this house."

Bertrand coughed and looked embarrassed before he rallied himself and said: "They say that a ghost may manifest itself by sound and even by touch whilst being invisible." The others nodded, encouraging him to go on. He looked at his wife nervously, as if for support. "After the Emperor died I could smell his orange-blossom cologne everywhere. I wonder, therefore, if a ghost cannot manifest itself also by smell?"

"Not you too, Bertrand!" Montholon cried. "You should be ashamed!"

Bertrand blushed.

Lady Lowe turned to him with the look of a mystic about to join hands around a circle, and said in a low voice: "I believe that queer odorous echoes *can* come surging up from past centuries to disturb the even tenor of our present life."

Bertrand nodded with a look of gratitude and embarrassment, and only then did Montholon let out a peeling laugh.

He sat back in his chair with a look of utter contentment and amusement. Then he took a long sip of wine and said: "The Emperor thought that we were all matter . . . that a man is only a more perfect being than a dog or a tree, and living better. The plant is the first link in a chain of which man is the last. After I am dead, the Emperor used to say, I will be quite happy if my body returns as a turnip or a carrot."

9

The repertoire of the ghost is neither wide nor broad. Once, it was enough to raise my bicorne hat for all of Europe to run to arms. Now all I could do was rattle doors, flick peas and blow up ladies' skirts. It was not a subtle way to communicate. My protests came like the rough raw acts of an infant who has not learnt his ABC, who shrieks rather than speaks, and has tantrums because he can't explain.

I was appalled by my courtiers. They had come to hear my will and had instead been distracted into trivialities and tittle-tattle. My pranks at the table – the peas, the air, the wine – had been misinterpreted and misconstrued. All in all they had been about as sensitive to my spirit as a pack of donkeys braying for food.

At last, however, when they had fed and watered themselves obscenely, Montholon – who I noticed had drunk far less than the others – began to take charge. "Perhaps we should begin, Sir Hudson," he said quietly; Lowe nodded, rubbed a hand over his pale freckled forehead, and stood up.

Lady Lowe ushered the party into a grand room with a marble fireplace and a small dog curled up in front of the fire. Vast gilt-framed paintings of podgy-handed monarchs and queens with elongated necks hung from the walls.

I looked around in irritation. There was not a waft of body odour, nor a whiff of excitement, indeed no air of anticipation

76

at all, that I could detect. The serving girls brought in coffee and brandy; the Governor asked Fanny where she acquired such excellent English; and Bertrand sat there like a stuffed poodle, stupid and replete, as if nothing more was anticipated than the opening ditty of a provincial band.

Montholon had moved to a small table in front of the fireplace, and was opening the black leather box, which had been placed upon it. Now - with a certain admirable flourish - he drew out my will and the eight codicils to it, each tied with a pink ribbon and sealed with my waxen crest. He held up his hand and, when everyone was silent, picked up the will and showed it to his audience, demonstrating that the seal was unbroken. Then, with a great deal of ostentation, he broke the wax, and folded out the first document.

He paused and looked up before he spoke. His eyes were aflame. *These are Napoleon's last words* - his eyes said - *his voice for one final time from the grave.*

I felt a thrill of impatience to see how those gathered would react! The magician revealing his hand after a slow six-year trick! I thanked the gods for awareness to witness it, and moved to where I could more easily observe their faces.

Montholon cleared his throat and began:

> *This is the last will and testament of Napoleon Bonaparte written in his own hand, this day 15th of April, 1821.*

He coughed hard a few times and began again:

> *I die in the Apostolic and Roman faith, in whose bosom I was born more than fifty years ago. I wish my body to be buried beside the Seine, in the midst of the people who have loved me so much.*

"Just a moment, Montholon," Lowe interrupted. "As I told you yesterday, I have had written instructions since 1819 that Bonaparte's body is, on no account, to leave the island."

Gourgaud looked at him with disbelief. "You are going to go on imprisoning *a dead man?*"

"Those are my instructions."

There was a pause in which Bertrand gave Gourgaud a warning look. Then the Grand Marshal began in his flat, reasonable voice:

"I believe it is customary in England that even the body of a common criminal is cut down and returned to his family after his death. Will you not extend this courtesy to the Emperor?"

"It is not up to me," Lowe replied, tightening his thin lips in a visible effort to remain calm. "The decision comes from His Majesty's Government."

"Is it *customary*," Gourgaud said in a disgusted voice, "for the English to go on torturing their victims even after death?"

"Please read on, Marquis Montholon," Lowe said, and surprisingly, without further argument, Montholon did.

I wish my body to be embalmed; my heart should be sent to my wife, Marie-Louise of Austria, and my stomach to my son.

"He cannot be embalmed," Lowe interjected.

"What?"

"Those are my instructions also. And the heart and stomach cannot be separated, but will be buried with the rest."

"And these too are England's instructions?" Gourgaud asked, incredulously.

"Yes."

"But *how* have you received instructions from England when no-one outside the island yet knows he is dead?"

"His death was anticipated."

"Was it?" Gourgaud said, raising his voice and beginning to shout. "And why was it anticipated? Because the English knew the island was unhealthy? Because they knew that isolation in this murderous climate would kill him? Yes, I can believe, they did *anticipate* it."

Lowe took a deep breath and said steadily. "Many eventualities were anticipated, including his escape." He looked around the room in a conciliatory fashion. "His Majesty's Government was changing its position on Bonaparte, you know. It was considering relaxing the conditions of his imprisonment, even of letting him return one day to Europe."

Gourgaud's face changed, and he suddenly looked as if he might cry. He said in a voice that was half-angry, half-pleading: "You tell us all this now and expect us to believe you? If it's true, why couldn't you have told us when the Emperor was still alive, when he might have been reanimated by hope?"

"These are my *orders*," Lowe said, beginning to sound frustrated. "You forget that I have no argument with you."

"So you keep saying. And yet you give us so many reasons to argue with you."

"Believe it or not, this is not a role that I ever sought. Or relished."

"And yet you have done it admirably, Sir Hudson. The role of turnkey suits you so well."

"You have hardly been under lock and key! You have had the use of thirty acres! The whole island if you wished!"

Gourgaud laughed, scandalised. "There have been sentries in our flower beds and under our windows at night!"

"How else could I be certain he would not escape?"

"Common sense might have told you!" Gourgaud shouted. "How could he escape when the sea is a moat fourteen hundred miles wide? One must be weak in the wits to imagine it possible."

"Bonaparte did not understand his position here, or else he was deceiving himself. He was not the guest of England; he was our enemy. An order had been given for his detention and it had to be carried it out." Lowe paused, opening and closing his mouth a few times like a fish.

Then he took a deep breath and started again in a quieter voice. "I am sorry that relations between myself and Bonaparte were not better, but, as you well know, that was his own fault. I have simply been following the instructions of my Government – my masters – just as you are now following the orders of Bonaparte. We can respect one another for that, can we not?"

"It's just so difficult to respect you, Sir Hudson, you who have always been so petty and so low! Your paranoia amounts to a disease, an itch that constantly requires something to scratch it! Did you not even confiscate the white and green beans *your own wife* sent us, thinking they might contain a semiotic code?" Gourgaud laughed wildly.

Hudson Lowe's freckled face blanched and his voice was very quiet as he said: "Once there was a monster stalking the continent of Europe, taking liberties at will. Now he is dead. And we shall not allow that monster's body to return to France, and stir the ambitions of others who seek to displace legitimate kings." Lowe stood up. "I should feel proud to have helped secure the man whose belligerence was once so fatal to the happiness of the world. Proud . . . ."

I was so furious with what I had heard that when Montholon finally resumed reading the will – after a prolonged argument on the hereditary rights of kings – it took me some moments to realise that the *order* of the will was not as I remembered it. Where I remembered writing detailed instructions for my son, he was reading the bequests to the Longwood party:

The following legacies are for my staff on St Helena. I leave five hundred thousand francs to Count Henri-Gatien Bertrand. I bequeath two million francs to Marquis Tristan Montholon to thank him for the filial devotion he has shown me in the

last six years, and to compensate him for the losses which he has
incurred during his sojourn on St Helena.

Why had I written 'filial devotion' when I had my own son?

I bequeath to Baron Gaspard Gourgaud six hundred
thousand francs and thank him for his tender care.

His 'tender care'? I never wrote that; I surely never wrote that?

To my valet, Louis Marchand, I leave the diamond necklace
that was given to me by Queen Hortense and once valued at a
million francs. The services he has rendered me have been those
of a friend.
I leave to Edouard Pierron, head of my kitchen, one hundred
thousand francs. These sums will be raised from the six mil-
lion francs that I deposited with Lafitte on leaving Paris in July
1815; and from the interest at the rate of 5 per cent since then.

Perhaps I have misremembered the order, I told myself. I *had*
been ill. But now it *must* be time for Montholon to speak of my
son.

Finally, I ask that my possessions on St Helena – my
jewellery, silverware, porcelain, furniture, books and weapons –
be divided equally between Marquis Tristan Montholon, Baron
Gaspard Gourgaud and my valet, Louis Marchand.
This is the final will and testament of Napoleon Bonaparte
written in my own hand this day 15th April 1821.

Montholon put down the papers.
It was all wrong . . . wasn't it? Where was the list of my possessions? The inventory of my snuff boxes? My Sèvres porcelain?

Where were the instructions stating that all my Longwood belong-ings – the saddles, the spurs, the bridles, the weapons – were left only in trust to my courtiers until they could be restored to my son? Above all, where were my . . . my prophecies, my instructions on how my son should regain the throne? I had only moments to observe the surprised expressions on the faces around the room before Montholon began reading again.

*This is the first codicil to the Emperor's will, written on the
16th April, in which he deals with legacies to his old soldiers.*

Over the next hour he went through the first codicils and the scores of legacies to my old faithfuls: what I had left to recompense the men who had lost arms and legs at Waterloo; the monies to be distributed to my Mameluke servants and to the exiles wandering abroad. Then he opened the codicils of April 24th and read of the hair bracelets to be distributed to my family; what I wished done for the 150,000 men who had lost limbs; and what for the two million widows. But nowhere . . . nowhere in all these rambling documents was there anything more about my son.

I could not understand it. I had been sick, I had had fevers, but I had been strong enough to write the will in my own hand, and to sign and seal the addenda myself.

I had said to my court, on April 14th: "Alors, I must pray for a few days of health so that I may put my affairs in order. If I die now," I added in a firm voice, "not one of you will be left a thing."

And miraculously, so it seemed, for the next ten days I had felt quite well, cool and temperate whilst I cast around through my life, evening up the score of regrets and wrongs, repaying all those who had served me well. I had dictated, inspected, and signed those codicils; I had sealed them and given them to Marchand, asking him to pass them on to Montholon. They had been in his posses-sion for the last weeks. Then I had gathered my courtiers to me and said: "Well, would it not be a shame to go on living having settled my affairs so well?"

They paled and cried: "Sire, only Your Majesty would have such a thought!"

Now I saw my son's image before me. His blond hair and smooth childish cheeks just as they had been the day I gave him his first tiny cannon and his first small sword. To think that my son was living with his Austrian mother in the country that had betrayed me; to think that a political marriage born of the desire to unite Europe had come to this! When I remembered how many years it had been since I saw him, I wanted to weep, because somehow, through some foul means, someone was trying to expunge the Bonaparte name . . . and what was to become of my son's future, of my grand plan, of *my dynasty*, without him?

10

I had been waiting in his room for two hours when I finally heard footsteps ascending the stairs.

Voices reached me. It was Lowe, no doubt, and the woman.

"I am surprised he has not left anything to his son or his wife," she said.

"You forget, my dear, he has left his son his stomach and his wife his pickled heart! What a generous gift to a far-away wife! Should I leave mine to you?"

She laughed. "No, dear, I don't think I should like it."

There was a pause, and a kissing sound before she went on: "What a strange business about the embalming. Do you think that they imagine if they embalm him, he'll still somehow live? It's like a heathen ritual: something you hear of happening among the Mandingos, not amongst us. Have they learnt nothing from the Church? Ashes to ashes, dust to dust?"

"I don't know . . . ." He made a strange sound as if he was shuddering. "All I know is the thought of that man remaining for perpetuity as he was on that billiard table fills me with disgust."

"What about the gravestone?"

"Gourgaud wants all manner of purple prose. Bertrand has been simpler. He wants: *Napoleon, born Ajaccio 1769, died St Helena 1821.*"

"Will you allow it?"

"He will be General Bonaparte or nothing. They refuse to call him General. We refuse to call him Napoleon or Emperor. Therefore they will inscribe nothing on it."

"An unmarked grave?"

"Yes. Obscurity. Of sorts."

"His means of death, his obscure burial, / No trophy, sword, nor hatchment o'er his bones, / No noble rite nor formal ostentation."

"Shakespeare?"

"Umm."

There was a pause. Then: "You must rest, my dear."

"I must. I'm very tired."

"You'll manage without Roberts tonight?"

"Yes. I didn't want to keep him late just to undress me. You forget that I was once a soldier."

"I don't forget, Hudson! Sleep well."

"I shall. Goodnight, my dear."

I heard them kiss, long sentimental sounds that chilled my heart. Why was my jailor permitted a wife? Why, when Bertrand and Montholon had been allowed theirs, had I been denied the solace of a wife's touch, and been reduced to the hard grind of self-use?

I waited for the door to open, but the kissing went on. At last, however, the goodnight sounds ceased and a moment later the door of the bedchamber was thrown open.

Lowe went to the long mirror and took off his sabre, looking at himself in the glass as he did so. He was not a fine figure of a man. Or, to be more accurate, his figure was good enough, was lean and long, but his high freckled forehead, the rough flakiness of his skin, and the unnatural yellow tinge of his complexion were astonishingly repellent. The thin red hair, the narrow nose, and the expression that alternated between fear and insolence in those too-close eyes were the crowning touches to a picture of repulsiveness.

He undid the gold buttons of his white jacket and removed it, then unfastened from each shoulder the epaulette with the red and gold braid of the diplomat. Underneath his jacket he wore a vest made of flannel – the sort you see common sailors wear to keep out the cold. He took off this too, and hung it up. Though he looked discordant in his uniform, like a plebeian dressed as an aristocrat, without it he looked younger, as if he might still take a new shape. But he was also defenceless . . . pregnable . . . .

He took a pale blue nightshirt from the armoire, went to the dresser, poured water from the jug into a bowl, and proceeded to wash himself, and never in my life have I seen a person – with the exception of Joséphine – wash so thoroughly. Every inch of his face and scalp was lathered in soap and water. He was careful to miss nothing, appeared to be entirely absorbed in his task – like a cretin lost in wonder at the pleasure of water. When it was over, and he had rubbed himself vigorously with a harsh towel, I knew the reason for his red and scaled skin: He had spent years trying to wash something away.

He blew out three candles, brought a fourth to his bedside, climbed under the sheets. It was a strange moment for me. While I was determined to exact my revenge and that this was the only way to do so, I was revolted to find myself sharing a bed with the man who had been my jailor, who had been the object of the largest part of my hate. The habits that had annoyed me at our very first meeting – his perpetual nose rubbings and endless clearings of the throat – were still there. Cough, cough, cough, he barked, and it meant nothing, one could tell. It was only a gesture left over from something else.

I thought he meant to sleep, but he, like me, sat upright in bed, and took from his drawer a notebook and quill. He turned immediately and with some avidity to the 5th of May and read his diary entry:

> Bonaparte died this morning. Bertrand informed me just after seven o'clock. It seems that his illness was not, and as I had so often suspected, an elaborate hoax. I rushed to Long-

wood House to see the body. There was some talk of refusing
me entrance until he had been washed, but I brooked none of it.
None of them can resist me now Bonaparte has gone; their will
has crumbled without him.

He chuckled, turned to a new page, scribbled 9th May 1821, and
underlined it with his quill. Then he began writing:

This evening Crokat left aboard the Acheron to take the
news of Bonaparte's death to England.
Charlotte and I, together with the entire French party, will
leave on the Camel, which set sail from the Cape last week and
should be here in a few days. It will be a strange nine weeks at
sea, all of us together.
Some of the divisions have already gone. Half the 55th
left yesterday on an Indiaman bound for Madras. The troops
seem relieved to be leaving. They cannot understand why they
have spent six years playing cards and hunting goats when they
were sent to guard the world's most dangerous man. "Bony's
let us down," one of them told me. This isn't the ending they
expected.
In a few weeks, all three thousand troops will be gone. Then
the island will be left to itself, with only an unmarked grave to
show the place where the bones of England's greatest enemy has
been 'laid to rest'. I cannot imagine – after his crimes – how he
can ever be at peace.

He put down his quill, blotted his words, and put away his book.
Then he blew out the candle, and I was alone in the dark with him,
my spine tingling with an exquisite vibration.
My senses were alive. They were. It made no difference that I
was dead, all my instincts and heightened night senses were shouting at me, making narrative out of sound and movement, telling

me how things looked, despite the blackness. I had a horror of Lowe touching me or moving his hand through me, but almost immediately he stopped clearing his throat, and his breathing steadied and, before I had had time to accustom myself to the possibility, he was snoring, fast asleep.

This wasn't how it should be! There was to be a tussle and a battle. I was to terrify him to death, not be the quiet partner in his quiet bed! With considerable effort and several attempts I was able to strike a match, and I held it to the candle hoping the light would wake him. But when he did not stir, it occurred to me that the cushion beside me might serve some other purpose than sleep.

I moved the pillow and began to slowly squash it over his face. Through the linen and feathers his breath seemed to labour, rasping as it moved in and out of his lungs. I tucked the pillow around his mouth and nose, then climbed upon it, bearing down with my squat weightless self upon the mass of his head. I sat there for many minutes, watching the slow rise and fall of his long thin chest.

As I sat there, I was filled with a glorious sense of revenge. He thought he was leaving did he? He thought it would soon be over? I whispered in his ear: *"The corpse of an enemy always smells sweet."*

It was he who had sent me to the wettest part of the island and given me the climatic fever that had made me so mad I had forgotten my son. Death? I had accepted that – embraced it even – knowing as I did its purpose in my legend. But what if there had been no point to my exiled suffering, but *suffering*? Had all my martyred attitudes led only to this? Had I gambled my life for a future that Lowe, with a few casual words, had spirited away? For with that autopsy report, no-one would believe me a martyr. And without my body back in Paris, none of my old comrades would fight. And without my organs, possessions and instructions for his future, my son would simply believe his father had died and forgotten him.

For what is a martyr without a body? How would my death help my son if it could not be seen? For such are the limitations of the common people that they cannot feel suffering unless they see it. My body had to be embalmed and set in a glass cage in the centre of Paris, where all could come and pay their franc to look upon genius. Only if my body was there, would I be remembered properly; only if I was there, could factions meet around me and plan the final destruction of the Bourbons; only if I was there, would my son be compelled to leave his Austrian family and come to pay his respects to his father; and only if I was there would he meet my family and have them correct the misapprehensions his mother's family would have taught him. Only the sight of my body could remind him that he had more Bonaparte in him than Hapsburg; remind him that he was a Napoleon in his soul, that military genius was his, that the dynasty begun by me was now his to continue. Only if the sight of the dead body of his father came as an affront, a most cruel death, a murder! Only then . . . For such are the defects of men's minds that a pile of earth and a flagstone mean nothing to them, but the sight of a face, an expression, a uniform and a sword is capable of inciting . . . anything! Everything!

I became carried away, sitting there. Although revenge is not in my nature, and I have forgiven many men who betrayed me, I could not find it in my heart to forgive this man, who, through sheer pedantry, was now ruining my plan. The glee with which he consigned me to an unmarked grave! The glee with which he insisted I could not be embalmed! The thought, the sight, the sound of him filled me with a high pitched hatred and I only wished that he have the worst, the most ignoble, the vilest end. Now, knowing that I would give it to him filled me with a great pleasure. I felt full of my own power. *Things are still possible*, I told myself. *A Napoleon can but rise and rise and rise.*

His breathing seemed to diminish further, and with every ounce of my strength I drained him of life. Sitting on his nose, struggling to define my mass and weight against him, I felt I was achieving my goal; I was sure of it indeed. But suddenly there were footsteps outside and a knock at the door. Lowe did not answer and I willed the presence away.

A soft voice outside whispered: "Hudson, my dear, are you still awake?"

When he did not answer, the stupid woman came in, knocked me effortlessly aside as she moved the pillow, and stroked his scaly head, saying: "Hudson, dear, you've fallen asleep with the candle burning and a pillow over your head!"

I willed the bitch to leave, to let him be, but he pulled the coverlets aside and said breathlessly, as if still in a dream: "Oh, my dear, join me if you will."

She picked up the skirts of her nightgown and climbed in, and, before I had chance to anticipate it, the candle had been snuffed out and I was between them, party to their night murmurings, their words of sweet content.

11

In the cool night air, slumped in an armchair in the moonlight, watching the sleeping bodies of the Lowes, I came to see that whatever else my jailor had done, he could not have altered my will. His instructions had affected my son's ability to reclaim my throne only by chance. The deliberate attempt to sabotage my dynasty came from an entirely different source.

There is only ever one small step between victory and disaster, and it is my experience that some minute detail always decides the issue. Now I resolved to look back over the course of events and find the detail that had undone my Resurrection.

The facts when I distilled them were these:

My body would not be permitted to return to France.
I would not be embalmed.
My will had been altered, and my son omitted.

The first two were, quite conceivably, instructions from a far away England. It made sense that England, my most lasting enemy, should wish me to rot. They would not underestimate the potency of my mummy in the middle of Paris, scant miles from their own shore. The Prince Regent had long feared a Bonaparte revival, and its kindred flame: a violent disgust for the hereditary succession of kings. The English royal family were wise to fear that the revolution that had led to headless French kings might spread to their land. Yes . . . *they* knew what Napoleon's dead body in the middle of Paris would mean.

The third matter, however – the effacement of the legacies and instructions for my son – I could not easily blame on the English, for they had had no access to my will. Only my own unhinged self could have undone, in the madness of dying, what my less frenzied self had secured. Or a member of my court, someone able to imitate my hand: an intimate.

Who had benefited from this altered version of my will? Montholon, Gourgaud, the servants. Who had lost? Bertrand. Fanny. My son. Had it been merely a question of money, the suspects would be clear enough, but it was not just a question of money – there had been a suppression of all that I had said to my son.

I had long considered that a smouldering personal resentment might put my life at risk. St Helena had offered my courtiers few financial benefits and little prestige. All that they could hope for was to dine out on the details of my decline and fall after I was dead. When they clamoured to accompany me, they did not expect me to stay: they had remembered Elba and assumed I would escape. They did not know that I had no intention of escaping. For where should I escape to? To America? To oblivion? To become just 'that man' who once ruled a Lilliputian foreign land? St Helena was the perfect place to choose to play the martyr; it provided the very best of tragic ends: a vast figure on a tiny island, severed from all he most loved. Prometheus chained to a rock with the British vultures pecking perpetually at his liver.

And so my followers had, to their surprise, found themselves poor in my court, without hope of a return to France, and only one thing standing between their imprisonment and their release: my life.

Had the simple desire for money motivated the desecration of my will, I believe I may have forgiven them. But what had now become clear was that someone had coolly and deliberately tried to destroy my dynasty, and stunt the future of my son. So I came during that long night in the moonlit armchair to ask myself the dreadful questions, the questions that I could no longer avoid: had I been more mad in dying than I seemed? Or had there long been an enemy lurking amongst my most trusted men? Even to ask these questions silently and in the dark hours sent a cold pulse of fear from the apex of my skull to the base of my spine.

12

Montholon is trying not to laugh. All evening he has been struggling to hold back a smile and only here, in the privacy of his own
chamber, can his lips curve away to expose his teeth. He has never
been good at this – there is something about mournful faces that
makes his lips twitch. He is uncertain whether he managed to hide
his mirth completely earlier in the evening, and he keeps remind-
ing himself of the importance of succeeding, but really everything
strikes him as so funny. Longwood is more than ever full of pomp-
ous people. Gourgaud screeching and squealing about this and
that, Marchand rushing around in despair like a dog without a
master, and Bertrand with a painted face of doom when one knew
that what he really felt was relief.

It isn't the time to say so, and pretence has subsumed them all
for so long, but how he longs to shout: "*Don't pretend that we haven't
all desired this!*" He can't pretend to feel grief. "*It is a tragedy for Europe!*" – well, yes, he can say all the right words. But for Montholon
the truth is clear: so many people wished the Emperor dead, that
eventually he was forced to concede.

He looks around the room as he takes off his shoes, and he can't
stop himself: he giggles at his good fortune. He alone has had
the stamina to go on as a courtier not as a man. Men are weak.
The exile has taught him this if nothing else. Men need affection,
women, freedom, prestige. Only he has sublimated himself fully,

paid that price, and received in return four-fold the investment of his suffering. It has, after all, worked out well for him.

Montholon puts on his dressing gown and sits by the fire. He has written his formal version of events already in his diary, but he now wants to amuse himself with a new drawing.

It will be a deathbed scene, of course. He has already drawn one of these for public consumption, but this one will be a little different. He will draw them as he saw them four days ago, standing around the bed: Marchand kneeling at the Emperor's feet, Bertrand's face bowed in grief, and Fanny and Gourgaud looking on with disbelief. He begins to draw the emperor, but this time he doesn't flatter him: the belly is not taut as it was in the earlier sketch, but mountainous; his face does not look grand or noble, but irritable and pinched. When he is happy with the Emperor, he starts on the courtiers. First he draws the sides of their faces turned towards the dying man, covering them with conventional expressions of grief; then, on the opposite sides of their faces, he paints laughter, huge smiles and open relief. He laughs, for isn't that an accurate depiction of everything that has been?

He blots his picture and flicks to the title page of the book – My Little Life by Napoleon Bonaparte – and imagines what the Emperor would have done if he had found this notebook when he sneaked into Montholon's room, instead of the one so thoughtfully left out for him.

Montholon stands up, stretches and laughs again. He laughs because it is all over, and because here, in front of him, is the return for his investment. The money bequeathed in the will means nothing, of course – the Emperor deluded himself in believing he had any assets left – but this last diary alone is worth a fortune! 15,000 sovereigns they have offered him in England for these few pages alone! 15,000! That would buy a house! A new title! A forest!

Hearing quiet footsteps along the corridor, he puts a hand over his mouth, and pushes the cupboard door shut.

The steps slow, falter and come to a stop outside his room. He moves quickly to cover the notebook still lying by the fire. Only Gourgaud would call this late, but those uncertain, light footsteps are not his. As soon as a hand taps tentatively at the door, he knows who it is. He puts on a dignified, mournful expression and at the third knock opens the door.

"Ma chère Fanny! What an unexpected pleasure."

She comes, tall and graceful, into his room and looks around, unsmiling.

"This is where you have lived?" she asks.

"Just here," he agrees. "Simple living."

"But where did Albine...?"

"She had the bed. A screen was here," he gestures. "And the little one, in a cot, here."

"But why did you not . . ." she pauses, and her cheeks colour.

He looks at her in expectation. After some time he says, "You must have known, my dear."

"Never. I never imagined it was so small."

"Don't delude yourself, Fanny. You were party to all the discussions when we first arrived. You saw our dismay. Albine's. Mine. Gourgaud's."

"I never thought it was so small."

"But, my dear, you could so easily have looked."

He enjoys her discomfort which comes six years too late and cannot repay him. He looks at her, and says in a voice loaded with sarcasm: "It was right that Bertrand, once Grand Marshal of the Imperial Palace, should have the sole independent house. Absolutely right, my dear, absolutely right. I was only head of the household stores."

She shifts uncomfortably, as if looking for a place to sit.

"I'm afraid there isn't a chair for you, Fanny, but Albine and I always found the bed comfortable in the long nights." He seats himself, and pats the bedclothes beside him, indicating where she should sit.

She sits as far away from him as she can, balancing uncomfortably on the corner of the bed.

"I am sorry to disturb you at such an hour."

"Can I help you with something, my dear? Have the events of the evening upset you? Do you want . . . ." He knows now what she has come for.

"Mon cher Tristan," she says with some effort. "You could help me, if you would."

"Anything I can do, Fanny, I will."

He leans forward and brushes a stray hair back from her face. His fingers linger as they smooth the strand behind her ear, and he enjoys seeing her discomfort, and knowing how hard she is trying not to flinch.

"The Emperor always said that he would treat us well . . . ."

"And so he did, my dear, so he did. What more wonderful way to repay us for our service than the honour of sharing his exile? I myself feel I will never be able to thank His Majesty enough."

"Tristan, you know what I mean."

"Mean?"

"Financial recompense. His Majesty always said that he would treat us well. But he didn't. Now, we are returning to France, to a place we no longer know, and Bertrand as you are aware . . . his health is not good." She pauses, faltering. "I am not certain how he will get a new position, for we shall certainly not be heroes under a Bourbon king."

"No, indeed, my dear. Our working lives seem very much over."

"Tristan, you know what I am asking. When did the Emperor alter his will?"

"Fanny, how am I to answer that? I am his executor only. We have none of us, before today, seen the will."

"Then who witnessed it?"

"No-one witnessed it."

"Then it is not legally binding in law."

Montholon looks at her and laughs. "Fanny, I know that your mother was English, but really! You seem to be talking of an English will. We French only require that it be written in the hand of the benefactor. That is quite sufficient in France."

"No witnesses?"

"No witnesses."

There is a pause. Then Fanny begins again.

"Do you think the Emperor was of unsound mind when he wrote it? He always promised to leave the diamonds to me."

"He was quite well when he wrote it," Montholon says in a firm voice.

"But is it not an odd thing . . . to leave a necklace to a valet? To keep the same will for six years, then rewrite it less than a month before death? He was delirious then, wasn't he? You can see it in the endless codicils, the mad handwriting . . . the ink splodges?"

"He hasn't had the same will for six years. He only left you the diamonds in his will of 1815. He has changed his mind – and his will – several times since then."

She wants to cry out in a loud voice, and let her screams fill the house. Instead she says in a sober voice: "Changed his mind?"

"Surely you knew that, my dear?"

She shakes her head.

"Well it seems to me that being so far away – and how far is your house, just a hundred metres over the green? – that you have missed out on a great deal. The smallness of our rooms . . . the will . . . ." He leaves his words trailing in the air.

"Were we left *anything* more in the penultimate will, Tristan? Please tell me. I don't ask for myself, you understand, but for Bertrand. He says he will not go back to Paris and approach a Bourbon king. He promised the Emperor. He talks of settling in a forest on a small estate. Tristan you must know what ideas he has."

Montholon paints on a questioning look.

"He says he will not see anyone but me. That he will have only women servants in the house . . . I am afraid . . . I am afraid that I am to be banished."

Montholon smiles, as if with sadness. His voice is deep and resonant as he says: "What a terrible end to such a beautiful woman – a woman whom the Emperor himself was said to admire. Was it true, my dear Fanny, that His Majesty importuned you?"

"Stop asking that. I have nothing to say about it."

"Nor I of the will."

There is a pause.

"Well, it seems we have reached an impasse."

Then, after a few moments: "Was it true that the Emperor told Bertrand he should prostitute you, and that your husband should make up your mind for you if you proved to be reluctant?"

"Tristan! I don't know where you get hold of such things."

"Are you regretting turning him down, Fanny, when you see what Gourgaud, Marchand and I have been left?"

She does not reply.

"Oh!" Montholon says, opening his eyes wide in fraudulent horror. "Are you regretting *accepting* him? Is that it?"

Fanny gets up, but does not speak.

"Ma chère, please, I am only joking. Have we forgotten laughter here? You want to know about the earlier will. D'accord. I did not, of course, read it, but I understand it left you nothing. Well, perhaps that is overstating it. Not nothing, but no useful amount. 600,000 francs or thereabouts, and I think I am right in saying he owed you 400,000? The Emperor, I believed, never liked the way you fed him soup."

Fanny flushes.

"If you feared losing his regard, why did you not alter your behaviour? Make yourself more pleasant? Sweeten your sour looks? Dine less often in your own house and more often in his?"

Fanny stands up and, without looking at him, asks: "Can I see it? Can I see that will?"

"It was destroyed weeks ago."

He stands and moves towards her, but she reaches behind, opens the door, and quickly steps outside. She says to him in her public voice, for it is always wise to think that someone might be listening at Longwood: "I came to tell you that the Governor will be here tomorrow at first light to pay the Emperor his final respects. He is coming with the coffin-maker."

"And if it isn't convenient for us in the morning?"

"He has made it clear we have no choice."

She takes another step back and looks him in the face. "Having seen the Emperor so seldom alive, he is determined to get the most from him dead."

He nods. "Then, we must have everything arranged well before dawn."

As she passes down the corridor, Montholon whispers loudly, "Fanny, does Bertrand know you have come to my room tonight?"

She turns and says quietly: "No. He would not like it, as you well know."

Avoiding the billiard room and the body, Countess Bertrand passes through the kitchen into the garden. Outside, the wind has dropped and the night air is warm and fragrant. She stops for a moment to confront her old enemy, the sky.

She does not know the constellations here: neither their patterns nor their names. In all her exiled years she has never allowed herself to become familiar with the southern stars. She has only glanced at the sky from time to time, shrunk from it, tried to ignore its endless aggression, its toneless criticism, endlessly repeated:

How insignificant you are, just the tiniest, tiniest particle of space! She has never known how to answer that sky or how to plead with it, how to beg that she – despite being tiny and insignificant – might be rescued from all this one day.

As a child she was told that when people died they became stars. Her mother had pointed out to her quite seriously, her great aunt Anna and her grand-father, Henri. The idea had comforted Fanny then, but now she is terrified that the Emperor is looking down upon her, spying again. She almost sobs as she scans the sky – *Is that him, that little star there?* And then her own voice: *Of course not, Napoleon will have to be the biggest, the very best.* She sees him there for a moment, Napoleon the newcomer, the brightest star, finally seated with Alexander and Darius and Caesar and Hannibal in the Kingdom of the Night.

She pulls her shawl around her shoulders and shivers despite the warm night. *Is he starting a war already?* she asks herself. *Does he still have a taste for battles to be fought?* She looks at the sky again and frowns, tries to push Napoleon from her mind, to remind herself that it is all over now, that she is released.

A silver-and-orange fish jumps and splashes in the half-moon pond. It is a sign to her that she should go and face the husband who has failed her. She must reach him now, before the night hours take him away from her, before he retires to catalogue his insects.

She stands for a moment staring at her house, then steps across the ha-ha, walks the hundred yards to her kitchen door, unlatches it and goes in.

"Henri-Gatien!" she calls softly.
"In here."

She closes the door carefully and follows his voice through the house. Her husband is in their tiny ballroom, sitting at a desk, examining crickets.

"Are they still there, Henri?" she asks affectionately. "They haven't hopped away during the evening?"

"Not much chance of that," he replies, gesturing to the pins with which he has just skewered an unfortunate creature, one of his latest finds. "Look, my dear, a new one. Have you ever seen such a vivid red?"

"Even the acacia seeds are not so red." She smiles at him and says in a teasing tone, "Henri-Gatien, I swear you have become an Englishman here with your insects and labels and preserving fluids!"

She picks up the bottle beside him and looks at its label: tincture of arsenic.

"Attention, chérie, it's open."

She puts it down, like a young girl chastised.

"How are the children?" she asks.

"They woke up when I came in. Arthur cried a little and wanted to play with his soldiers. But Hortense and Henri just drank their milk and went back to sleep."

"I think we should not have allowed Arthur to see the emperor."

"Perhaps not," Bertrand smiles wryly at the memory. "But he asked. Tomorrow he'll be back playing hide-a-seek with Pierron in the ha-ha, and catching insects in the garden, and it will all be forgotten."

Fanny nods, and looks at the tincture of arsenic again.

"Can't we embalm the body ourselves," she says, gesturing to the bottle, "despite what the English say? Gourgaud thinks we should, that France may want him one day."

"It's no easy matter, Fanny."

"You have done it with birds and crickets and tincture of arsenic."

"A human body is not quite a cricket."

Bertrand draws forth a label and begins to writes in his copperplate hand, *Class: Insecta, Order: Orthoptera....*

Fanny looks impatiently around the tiny ballroom. This is the room she had built in 1818, when she thought they would be here forever; the same year the Emperor built his ornamental garden. She had wanted the room for dancing and quadrilles; she had imagined laughter, swirling skirts and gay flirtations. Little by little, however, it has become filled with Bertrand's glass cases of dead things. The "small corner" that Bertrand had at first requested had grown slowly but consistently into a wall, then a wall and two corners, until at last Bertrand had forgotten that the ballroom had any other purpose than to display his dead creatures. Now, it was only with difficulty that one could step around the room.

"Where have you been at such a late hour?"

"Next door." She takes a deep breath. "I have seen Montholon."

"Yes?"

"I went to his chamber."

"Was that necessary?"

"I wanted to catch him alone. I asked him about it: when the new will was made; what the old will said."

Her husband puts down his label and turns towards her with a frown. "Was it necessary to be so crude, Fanny? Could we not have waited for things to take their proper course?"

"We let things take their proper course earlier this evening. If we had known the contents of the will yesterday, tonight should not have been such a hideous surprise. I should not have had to paint on a blank face whilst feeling close to fainting away."

"There's no need to be so dramatic."

"Henri," she hisses with anger, "it's been *six years!* Even you, with your noble sentiments, must feel we are owed *something.*"

Bertrand is silent. He sits for some minutes with his head bowed, so that the candlelight catches the shiny spot on his skull where his hair is thinning. *He is becoming bald,* she thinks, *he is thinning,* and the words hiss and spin in her head with all the melodrama of a bad line in a bad play. *My husband is getting old,* she thinks . . . *has got old . . . is fading away.*

The smell of the insects disgusts her, and she turns away impatiently.

At her movement, Bertrand raises his head.

"Alors, ma chère, at least tell me. What did he say?"

"Rien!" she hisses and then, quietening herself, "absolutely nothing. He said Napoleon had decided not to leave me the diamonds long ago. He said he did not know the contents of the previous will, but he was gloating, as if he wanted me to know that he did."

Bertrand's thin lips press together, and a strange look crosses his face. "It seems we have been out of favour for longer than we thought."

"It is my fault. The Emperor never forgave me for asking to leave with Albine."

"It is a blow for us both, my dear, but we must struggle to survive it."

"For all you think of me, Henri, it is not even the money I care for." Her voice quavers as tears spring to her eyes. "It is . . . the *insult.*"

"It is very wrong," her husband agrees. But he does not go to comfort her immediately. Before he goes to her, he will fit his box with its glass plate, place the lid on his ink well, and move his quill to its rest. But when he has finished these tasks, he finds she is gone.

Bertrand puts aside his boxes and allows his face to relax into the pattern of relief that he has all day hidden, out of habit, out of respect. Now he allows the seed of excitement to grow within him, the thrilling knowledge that soon, in less than three months, he will see his beloved country again, step once again onto his beloved France.

Despite his growing excitement, he finds himself troubled. Not only by his relief, which he feels dishonours him, but by the thought of Gourgaud sitting again with the body tonight. When he thinks of Gourgaud watching, he cannot imagine him standing upright, his face towards the Emperor, his hands behind his back, marching a few paces every twenty minutes or so: a parade soldier, as he, Bertrand, would have been. But he is glad to abdicate the burden of watching, for it has been a long time watching for all of them – six years of duty and a care for every expression on the face, and it has become harder to look admiring as the Emperor grew older, more than a year for each year that passed, here on the island. No, he doesn't imagine Gourgaud watching as he would have done, but he is relieved of the task, and therefore tries to avoid enquiring into Gourgaud's motives. After all, the Emperor *is* dead. This faint disquiet is just the nervousness of obtaining freedom after so long a wait, the mind playing tricks, as if to hang on to old worries, now gone, for in their sudden disappearance there is a vacuum, and a vacuum is frightening, and insists on being filled up.

He puts the lid on the bottle and snaps his last case shut. In his uncharacteristic haste, a wing of some tiny creature is trapped and turned to dust. He places the case down and stares at it. One of the *Drosophilae* from Yon's orchard – a common enough thing. Aside from these insects, this catalogue, Bertrand feels as if he has lost his ability to act. He feels as he imagines an actor does who – having played the same scenes night after night – is suddenly called upon to ad lib, to make things up. He is still surprised that the Emperor has not left exhaustive instructions for the days ahead. He would like to be told the procedure for mourning: the correct number of fallen tears, the proper number of salutes.

In the kitchen, Fanny is warming milk. She looks at herself doing this, and thinks for the thousandth time how extraordinary it is that life – her life – should come to this. That she should be forced to heat her own evening milk! It would hardly surprise her now if Bertrand bought a goat and called upon her to service it.

She is furious with her husband, with his passivity and calmness. She married thinking he was good for her – his coolness to her warmth, his dryness to her flame – but now Bertrand only increases her hysteria with his long careful hands, his thought-out phrases, his diary writ in hieroglyphs and codes.

She hears his slow, careful footsteps, and tenses as he comes into the kitchen.

"Is there milk for me too, my darling?" he asks, coming to stand behind her, putting his hands upon her shoulders. Such a simple gesture would once have calmed her, helped her to bear anything, now she only wishes to shake off his touch.

"Of course. But I thought you would want brandy."

"The events of the last days have affected my stomach."

He watches her standing over the stove with her back to him; admires her graceful movements – the elegance of her back, her long neck.

"We will manage," he says. "If Gonchor is still there, we can retrieve some of the furniture and the silver."

"We have no idea whether he is even alive. And if he is, he may have converted back to the monarchy. From what the guards say, everyone now supports the Bourbons or the Orléans. It's only we who are out of step with the march of France. We've lost everything."

"I'm sure the news will not be as bad as that."

"But how do you know, Henri? Where do you get your news? From the *Literary Survey* or the stories in the *Macclesfield Times*? You know no more of France than I do." She chokes back her quivering voice, and assumes an icy cool tone. "Don't pretend that we haven't gone up in flames. Everything is lost. If only you'd listened to me, when I said we should not come."

There is no answer to this argument, which has rumbled on over the years. This is just the last and bitterest phase.

"We could contest the will."

"No, Fanny, we could not."

"I shall never say a good word about him in Europe. How can I, after what he has done to us?"

"If you are wise, you will say only good things, because that is where our fortune now lies."

"Gourgaud says he has been offered 8,000 sovereigns for his diaries in London. Yours would be worth even more. Montholon is in charge of the kitchen and Gourgaud the stable, but Count Bertrand is still Grand Marshal of the Imperial Palace. It is a title for life."

"I shall not publish them. Unless you insist."

"When have I ever been able to insist upon anything?" she shouts. Then her voice trembles and breaks and she says pitifully: "It's not fair. Why should we be punished for wanting to leave the island? It's no secret that everyone wanted to leave Napoleon in the end."

13

I found the town easily, of course. After a long downward journey along steep paths cut into the hills, zigzagging by necessity like a vessel beating against the wind, I came to the top of a staircase hundreds of feet high, carved into the cliff.

Standing with a hand on either side of the rails, I looked down on Jamestown. There was little life on the stark brown hills that framed the island's only town, aside from a few goats, balancing at airy heights and munching on the meagre vegetation. Huge rocks perched perilously on either side of the ravine – boulders hanging at impossible angles and threatening destruction on the inhabitants beneath. The impression was one of utter aridity relieved only intermittently by the green of an almond tree, or the red bloom of a hibiscus, or the dark blue Atlantic. Nothing could be seen in the ocean's faceless expanse except a few ships and the shadows of sharks cruising the bay. But I knew that four thousand miles to the north was France.

At noon, after another hour tip-toeing along goats' paths, I entered the town from the top of the valley. The mile-long main street to the harbour took me past men smoking pipes on hospital verandas, past shopkeepers leaning in sunny doorways, past strangled chickens lying limp in the shade. Further down, dark children ran about wildly, firing at each another with peashooters; below them was the Poor House, the House for Incurables, and a shop in which a tall turbaned woman was cutting a length of grey silk for a soldier in red. I passed a courtyard full of bougainvillea vines, their bright purple petals blown into piles by the breeze and then . . . suddenly, mayhem! . . . the door to a tavern burst open and English soldiers in scarlet, black and gold poured out onto the street from the smoke-filled interior, blinking in the bright sunlight, laughing, hiccupping, slapping backs and belching their hot steam.

Opposite the Consulate Hotel, groups of soldiers were sprawled around smoking. Flags from the different maritime nations hung from the poles of the hotel and they, together with the jacks of the ships in the bay – whalers, merchantmen and men-of-war – conspired to give the town a festive air. I stepped around children begging red coats for chaws of liquorice and walked towards the water, wondering how I would change the world again and communicate all that I knew.

On the wharf, a great hubbub of humanity had gathered, and, though each man seemed absorbed in his own thoughts and deeds, there was some common feeling that seemed to unite them. At first I tried to ignore the emotion that quivered in the air. But in the end I could not but accept that it was joy, and I could not but realise that my death was the source of that joyfulness. There was not a single black armband in town and not a single wet eye.

Standing behind two beefy soldiers incongruously squashed together on the town's little kissing seat, I overheard them discussing why I had not escaped.

"Well, 'e never tried did 'e?" one concluded.

"Perhaps Bony were never as good, as they said," the other mumbled in a gin tongue. "Never was convinced about that bastard."

There was nothing I could do on the wharf, so I retraced my steps, crossing back over the small moat and through the town gates. I walked past little shops selling arrack, bolts of muslin, and feather fans; past a man sitting in the sunlight with dripping hair waiting for the barber to begin. I passed a negress with her hair wrapped in red cloth, her eyes the colour of walnuts; I passed Hindus in turbans and Chinamen with pigtails; I passed Mohammedans and Negroes, one of whom carried a little white boy in a basket who was slapping him on the shoulder and shrieking: "*Faster! Faster!*" As the sun's rays fell upon the English soldiers, their bayonets and rifles glinted like semaphore, and it seemed to me that there was a message in those flashes if only I could decipher it.

There, in the town, I proudly saw how many soldiers there had been; how they had overwhelmed and dwarfed the island's population. They were everywhere, making preparations to leave: galloping and charging around with laughs and shouts, paying old bills or seeking to escape them, making amorous farewells. The town was alive with a carnival atmosphere. They were sitting in the Botanical Gardens laughing at minstrel shows, playing cricket, catching fish off the rocks, swimming in the bay.

Once, these thousands of soldiers must have been watching – perched on cliffs as look-outs, or with telescopes straining out to sea – now they wore holiday faces and were released. In the town, the infrastructure of my imprisonment stood abandoned; the guns and cannons were unmanned and their balls stacked in unmoving pyramids. Two frigates criss-crossed the bay in figures of eight, but without military purpose: they were flying kites from their afterdecks. Not a single soldier still carried his bayonet with martial vigour, as I – invisible as Henry V on the night before battle – moved silently and purposefully amongst them.

Sitting in the shade of mango trees, old ladies were weaving baskets and lace handkerchiefs. A minter was selling coins with my face on one side and 'St Helena 1815-21' on the other. Away from the main street, in the doorways of pink and blue plastered houses, and along dusty goat paths darkened by the overhanging cliffs, men stood around hawking goods to passing soldiers.

"Pssst!" one of them hissed from a gloomy doorway. "Want summat to take 'ome for yer family?"

"Like what?" a passing red coat asked, drawing himself up like a schoolboy, proper and precise.

The old man took out a jar from beneath his cloak and held it towards the soldier: "D'ya know what this is?" he rasped.

The soldier's face changed: became white, then grey. He looked around furtively.

"What is it?"

"The manhood of an emperor," the man in the doorway said, with a low chesty rumble of a laugh. I looked closer.

"How did you get it?"

"Let's just say one of the surgeons who done the autopsy is a mate of mine."

"Can you authenticate it?"

"Want me to ask that Mrs Bertrand if she recognises it?"

"Of course not," the soldier said irritably. "But can you give me any evidence?"

"Now I hardly think the doctor will want 'is name known around town, now will 'e?" the relic-seller said with a cackle that reverberated around the doorway.

"But can you guarantee it is what you say it is?" the soldier asked, lowering his voice to a whisper.

"I can, sir. I can."

The soldier withdrew from his pocket three ducatoons, and pressed them into the man's hand. Then he took the jar with its wrinkled piece of goat's flesh, thrust it deep inside his bag, and hurried up the street.

I stood there a little longer. The relic-seller counted the coins with dirty fingers. Then, satisfied, he placed them in his purse and turned his eyes back to the street.

"Pssst!" he hissed at a man who was passing alone. "D'ya want a li'ul souvenir to remember your time 'ere?"

He drew from a battered leather bag another object: "Preserved in tincture of arsenic, it should last forever." Then, with a look of abominable malice, he drew out three teeth and what looked to be - on close inspection - a sheep's stomach wrapped in a pocket-handkerchief.

Away from the light of the main street, along the narrow lanes, there were scraps of my autopsy sheet, shreds of my stockings, and leaves from my gum trees on sale. All down the back alleys, a vigorous exchange: *Buy yerself a relic! Remember what Bony has been!*

I was not sickened by what I saw, for these acts were an indication of the great things to come: a sign that everything I had worked for might actually come to pass. In packing cases throughout the island - placed in bottles, caskets and jars - were parts of me, and random things I had touched, for everything connected to me had gone up in price. There were trees in Jamestown on which centuries ago people had carved their names, and, as the trees had grown so had their names, becoming larger with each year. So it would be with me - if only I could communicate what I knew.

I had overheard a soldier saying that a frigate was leaving for Europe that afternoon, and, remembering the necessity of getting my letters onto that ship I entered the Consulate Hotel and climbed the narrow wooden staircase to the writing room. I hadn't been there since my first night on the island; then, as now, though the town was tumultuous, the little writing room overlooking the street was quite deserted. I tried to pick up a quill – tried again and again until at last my hand was able to keep its own borders and that of the feather distinct. Then I dipped the nib in the ink pot and, with great difficulty, began:

St Helena, 9th May 1821

My dear son,
  I hope this letter reaches you in Austria, but since I have not heard from you for six years, I am not convinced that it will.

I started again.

Mon cher fils,
How can I expect you to believe this is a letter from your father? The date must make it seem a hoax.

The soldiers on the street outside broke out laughing, and I saw one of them grab a whore and lift up her skirts.
  I started again:

Son, this is your father writing. The date is April 1821, and I am dying. Will you believe this shaky hand is mine if I remind you of the secrets that we shared: remind you that the cannon I gave you when you were three was a replica of my own first artillery cannon; the sword a replica of Sobieski's; that I had your little soldiers painted blue by the men of the Imperial Guard? Do you remember the lace that I had made for your toddling clothes, by Aunt Joséphine's friend whose name was R–p–r–y? Only I know that name which was your secret word for britches

113

– do you remember calling them that as a child? I am fearful to write more because I do not know what will happen to this letter even if I can get it aboard the frigate.

I stopped, sighed and began again.

Joseph, I wrote, *Brother,*
I have loved power. Loved it as a conductor loves his orchestra, for the chords and harmonies that can be drawn from it. But now the conductor is dead.
I once wrote and told you that the English were killing me on St Helena, a letter to which you did not respond. But it is not the English I fear now; it is the French. I took everything from them – their sons, their wealth, their labour – offering in return glory, but failing in the end to give them glory, sacrificing them for my own ends, in a last effort to ensure the everlastingness of my own name.
Someone has betrayed me. And he is French. Someone I have lived with for six years. I have always had to sow at a gallop, and sometimes I fear I have cast my seed onto sandy or sterile ground. Perhaps I have been too occupied with heavy thoughts . . . the weight of my crown. I have carried the world upon my shoulders, a fatiguing task. I need you now as I have always needed you. I am Samson, blind in the temple, deserted by my Delilah, and no strength to bring the temple down.

I put the quill down and re-read the letter. Oh God!

Dear Mother,
You must calm yourself, but something terrible has happened. My will has been forged, and I do not know by whom. These are the people who had access to my will: Montholon, Bertrand, Marchand and Gourgaud. You must find out who has done it. Why have you not written to me, Mother? Why did you send me

an anatomist when I requested a doctor? Why did you send me that young fool Antommarchi? Why did you not come?

Chère Hortense,
    You gave me your necklace in case I ever needed it, and now I do. Forgive me, I, who in the past, have been so generous to you. I have left six million francs with Lafitte, and the income from that should be 5%. You must make sure these monies go to my son, so that he can be independent of Austria. Draw him close, Hortense; keep him away from his mother. Remind him who he is; who his father is: make me real in his mind. Tell him that he is French to the fingertips, tell him power is never ridiculous, that war justifies everything; tell him nothing is beautiful unless it is vast; that in China the sovereign is adored as God, and that is how it should be.

Mon Dieu! To have a son and be unable to guide him!

Joseph,
    Perversity is always individual, scarcely ever collective. Joseph's brothers could not agree to take his life and it was Judas – cold, hypocritical and with dastardly calculation – who delivered his master unto death. So it must have been here – one betrayer, not all.
    The things I have said about the Bertrands are not true. I have been jealous of their conjugal love. Fanny, too, has . . . taunted me, looking so much like Joséphine. But only Bertrand has always been there, through victories and failures; only Bertrand, always seeing, always submitting.

Bertrand,
    Forgive me for the insult of the will. And the insults before then. This is how life is: sometimes you are most bitter towards the ones who have done the most.

115

But I have one last duty for you. And you must fulfil it.

Everything is not as they say. Death is not oblivion or forget-fulness. Death is something else entirely. My dear Bertrand, this is me! Recognise my hand, and know that it speaks the truth.

The will that Montholon read out at Plantation House was not mine. I do not know how or why, but I leave you to discover the truth of what has happened: you, my oldest, most trusted friend. Can I say friend, Bertrand? Forgive me, forgive the anger, the tantrums and deliriums of a dying man, and accept the truth from a dead one. The truth is, Bertrand, that I can see you, and you cannot see me. I can see the secret processes of men. I can look into your soul and see that it is clear, without a shadow or cloud. I see you for what you are: noble, dignified, depressed. I see Fanny for what she is: excitable, flighty, loving. But I cannot see what Montholon is, or Pierron, or Gourgaud. I cannot get close. What has happened to my will? Look at who has benefited: 2 million to Montholon, 600,000 francs to Gourgaud, the diamond necklace to Marchand. Who has eradicated all the bequests to my son? Who wants to punish him and me and you?

Bertrand, you have served me as a lesser man must a greater. Do this last thing, and you will rise and we shall walk through Elysium holding hands together. Bertrand! Do this for me! I charge you –

At that point, the quill fell from my fingers and I was unable to pick it up. I tried again and again, but my grip had gone and the edges of the quill gave way like water. It was only when I sat back in my chair in despair that I realised that the noise outside had died down, and when I stood to look out of the window, there were no more men having haircuts, no negroes, no Chinamen, the shops were closed, and the streets were emptied of civilians. I must have been in a trance when I was writing, for what I saw now on the street astonished me: as far as the eye could see there were soldiers lined up in ranks of twenty broad, all glistening bayonets, golden buttons, leather belts and red wool.

Suddenly, a choir began to sing. It was an unearthly sound, so clear and high that even the doves seemed to recognise that they were out-sung and stood silently looking on from the roof tops. Then the drums began to beat, a slow, rumbling thunder that increased as the minutes passed until finally, at a cry from the front, the procession began moving slowly up the hill. I stood on the balcony watching as line after line of red coats passed below me. From my angle, high above the street, they looked like tin soldiers, like three inch men - priests, choirboys, trumpeters, dragoons, infantry, cavalry, artillery, drummers - all with blank faces like toys carved to an identical pattern. To the slow beat of the drum, they passed below me, a blood-red stream of men, and so mesmerising was that sight to an old soldier that it was only when the last man had passed and I saw the stragglers at the end - the rabble of island children and women dressed in their Sunday best - that I realised what was happening: after four days, they were going to bury me.

Forgetting the letters, I ran down the stairs to take my place in the ranks. *An expedition can be led from behind*, isn't that what Ney used to say? That my presence on the field could make the difference of 40,000 men? Well, it was my funeral and I was leading again, and this time from the rear.

I will never forget that walk across the island to the slow beat of the drums. There had been so much monotony on the island, that the sight of a pageant - even if it was the one to mark my death - soothed me. And as we wound our way up the steep mountains, snaking our way around the bends for what seemed like hours and hours, I began to know St Helena for the first time. St Helena had always appeared to slumber. Now she seemed to raise herself on one arm dreamily to observe the strange procession of human ants crawling over her ribs. She did not move to brush us off, or throw us - with one arch of her back - to the ocean floor. She lay there on her side, leaning her head upon her arm, a lone eyelid raised, watching us with amused curiosity, for had she not spent three hundred years observing the bizarre antics of men?

On that march, I began to know St Helena: her spirit of tolerance, her black basalt columns rising hundreds of feet into the air, her pomegranates and orange trees, her wetlands and wild watercresses, her heart-shaped waterfall, the observatory where men were studying the southern stars, and I began – how strange is the nature of the human heart! – to love my old prison on that journey towards my end.

As we neared the gates of Plantation House, the procession halted for a few minutes in the shade of a eucalyptus forest, and waited until Lowe and his wife appeared in a calabash drawn by six black ponies. Then the procession moved forward again, winding up and up through the lush interior, through forests of giant ferns and vast hanging flowers, past hills and valleys I had never seen.

Now the soldiers could no longer walk in broad formations, but only four abreast along narrowing paths, so that the snake of the procession grew thinner and longer. And, as the cortège drew near the head of a valley, some of the English troops formed an avenue between which the rest of us passed, and we headed towards a stream and dark green willow trees and geraniums lush and red. The priest and the drummer boys halted, a bugle sang out and – emerging from the shadow of the willow trees – I saw my courtiers standing with heads bowed before an object: it was the mahogany of my coffin.

I looked along the dark line of my mourners: observed Bertrand's taut lips, Gourgaud's sunken eyes, Montholon's pale anxiety, and Marchand's face, grey as if he had been beaten since dawn. The children were sobbing and Fanny Bertrand – even Fanny Bertrand – stood there with a mist of nostalgia in her eyes.

I thought then that even if my son was not here, even if Joséphine and Marie-Louise were absent, and my parents, siblings, nephews, generals and soldiers were far away, my courtiers *were* mourning me, there *was* sadness in their eyes, and my passing had caused genuine sorrow for this one woman, these few children and men.

Such was my illusion for a moment, until I remembered every-thing I had discovered since my death. An image flashed through my mind then: it was December and the sun was shining as I was driven in a gold carriage through the Notre Dame crowds. I saw the children sitting on their father's shoulders to catch a glimpse of me, the tumult of thousands crying: Vive l'empereur! Vive l'empereur! What had those cries come to? I asked myself now in despair.

Nothing has any permanence. Rootedness is a fallacy and belong-ing a myth. All my great works, everything I had done, all the chang-es I had brought to France and the world, would in their time fade, and not a single law or principle or practice of mine would remain.

A pair of tortoises had started mating in the bushes, and the loud clack of their shells broke the air intermittently, as Father Vignali began to intone the Mass for the Dead: "*Subvenite Sancti Dei, occurrite Angeli Domini, Suscipientes animam ejus, offerentes eam in conspectu Altissimi.*"

An immense faintness came over me. This is it, I said, the mo-ment when consciousness finally passes. My legs gave way and I sat down on the grass. I had no voice, no will. I was not an actor, not even a reactor, but a passive observer now, nothing more. Would I lose all awareness when the coffin was in the ground? Become a spirit complete? I did not know. I opened my mouth to ask the soldiers to stop, but no sound came out. So what could I do? I merely watched as my body, inside its four coffins, was lowered into the ground.

I stayed there for countless hours, long after the last mourners had left, lying on the damp earth watching the birds wheel and skit-ter overhead. At some point an unfamiliar creature, some sort of hook-beaked bird of prey that I had never before seen on St Hele-na, came and perched on a branch above me, its talons closed tight around the branch, its heavy head on one side, the large pupils of its golden eyes fixed on some far away thing. Then it too flew away.

14

"Well, the weather was beautiful," Dr Chapman says, pushing his way through to the table. "It quite transformed the island to have its little roads covered with people and its hills filled with musicians."

His colleague, Surgeon Henry, nods and follows him through the crowds of English officers.

"It seemed to go off well," Chapman continues, reaching a small gap. "Difficult balance to achieve, I think. Respect without pomp. In the circumstances, I think the Governor managed rather well."

They are standing in the dining room in Longwood House trying to reach the table. Pierron has been roasting for two days to produce this tottering tower of food, this repast, this Massif Central of partridge, pheasant and fish. On the table next door are tarts and pastries and Pierron's tour de force: a spun-sugar sculpture of the Emperor's favourite palace, Fontainebleau, complete with grazing deer.

"I don't know what it is about a funeral that makes one so damn hungry."

"It was a long walk. Twelve miles, I should say."

"Do you think anyone will notice if we have a nibble?"

"Probably not," says Henry looking around. "The French are speaking to the chief islanders next door."

The afternoon sunshine casts trapeziums of light on the floor and the green walls gleam like emeralds. Chapman shuffles towards the table, pulls the wing off a quail and begins to crunch.

"Yes, I think the Governor did rather well in the circumstances. Had problems with Antommarchi, I understand. Try this quail, Henry, bloody delicious! Apparently, he had a devil of a time getting him to sign the autopsy report."

"Why?"

"Said he couldn't in good conscience sign the report if it didn't include his opinion that the liver was enlarged. Damn!" Chapman exclaims, seeing a splatter of fat and a splinter of bone drop onto his waistcoat.

"Well," he continues, "it's rather easier for him to object. I myself pointed out to His Excellency last week that Antommarchi's observations had been left out of the official report and the Governor told me in no uncertain terms that any Englishman who was heard even *speaking* of an enlarged liver would be court-martialled, suspended without pay, and probably at risk of dishonourable discharge." He finishes his quail and wipes his hands on a handkerchief. "Not easy to accept at my age," he says, eyeing a peacock. "Well, it's only disputes about trifles. The findings were clear enough . . . . Still, I suppose if one wanted to split hairs, one could question the cause of the canker." He smiles. "Perhaps it was even poison of the soul!"

The two surgeons laugh.

"I'm sure that's just the sort of thing Bonaparte hoped you might say."

"Still, if we didn't know the hereditary factor, the cause may have been more complicated to establish. The symptoms were certainly very strange . . . very strange with cancer not to have *some* wasting of the body. There must have been two inches of fat over the heart and omentum, wouldn't you say?"

Henry looks around the room, then lowers his voice conspiratorially: "Madame Bertrand once told me that Bonaparte was exceedingly careless about what he ate. She said that some days he drank as many as twenty cups of coffee, and always thick and bitter. Imagine that!"

Chapman nods, his lips pursed in a disapproving line. "Antommarchi said the same. His habits were not healthy: too little mastication, too short a time at meals. They say he liked only bread soaked in wine at the last." He raises his eyes incredulously.

Henry laughs. "He was a Frenchman. I suppose his digestion was used to it. Wine for the French invalid, roast beef for the English."

"I know which I should prefer."

"That's my point, Chapman, your system has been brought up on roast beef. I think a man can tolerate anything if he's been fed it since birth. The things that shock the body are the novel and the new. I suppose a cannibal would turn quite green on seeing a parsnip."

They laugh again.

"The hairlessness of the corpse was a strange thing, though. Only ever seen it in syphilitics who have been too long on arsenic."

"Hairlessness?"

"Did you not notice that none of his fine body hair remained?"

Henry, embarrassed by his failure to observe this, says hurriedly: "Perhaps he *was* syphilitic. I should certainly imagine the French would want to keep that quiet. One can't blame them for that. But from what Antommarchi *deigns* to tell us of the symptoms of his illness, they seem pretty conclusive of cancer. Pain. Lethargy. Headaches. Nausea. Chills in the legs. The usual sort of thing."

Chapman nods, then raising his voice as he sees Montholon pass by: "Yes, certainly a fine day for it." Then in a whisper: "They say he used to work for the Bourbon king. That his brother still does. That what he inherited from Napoleon was compensation for what was done to his wife."

Henry leans forward.

"They say that Bonaparte had *no money* left to bequeath; that he bestowed with the munificence of an Emperor, yet owned less than a pauper. At the end he was like one of those poor lunatics in Bedlam, who with rags and dirty feet fancy themselves kings."

"It went off very well," Bishop Warden says kindly. "Very moving, the bugle in the Valley of Silence."

Bertrand nods, strokes Arthur's head, but does not reply.

"May the animosity between England and France be buried with him."

Bertrand nods again glumly. "Thank you. Thank you for your kindness."

There is a silence. Warden looks around. "If it is not impertinent to ask, Count Bertrand, may I ask you for the great man's last words?"

"He said: *Orgeat, orgeat.*"

Warden looks at him blankly.

"He wanted a drink."

Warden stares at him, disappointed.

Realising this is not enough, Bertrand adds: "Then he said: *La France, tête de l'armée, mon fils.*"

At Warden's blank look, Arthur translates in his high childish voice: "That means France, head of the army, my son."

Warden nods and looks pleased, but silence soon returns. Seeing the bleak face of Bertrand before him, he searches for something appropriate to say.

"What will you do now?" he asks at last.

Bertrand tries to think of an answer. But he thinks as a man whose mind has been occupied by one subject for six years. Now

– with the departure of that subject – he finds his own mind cut adrift. He understands that in the months to come he will have to find new matter to fill his brain, but as yet he has no idea what that will be. Even now he finds it impossible to oust the figure who has settled and feathered itself into the nest of his brain. Standing in the small drawing room, tentatively exploring the forgotten contours and spaces of his mind, he finds that wherever he reaches, Napoleon appears.

Warden is looking at him expectantly, waiting for an answer.

Bertrand wants to confess: *I am just a shadow; an insipid imitation of my old self; I have no plans for an emperor-less future.* But in the end he just shakes his head and says: "I really don't know."

"Whatever torments you have suffered here," Warden says gently, "will have some greater purpose."

"I hope to believe that."

Bertrand looks over at his wife, surrounded by a group of English officers, and the Emperor's words come back to him: "*Your wife is a whore. She goes with the English soldiers. I have even found her in ditches with them.*"

"Excuse me for a moment, Bishop, if you will. Arthur, come."

Countess Bertrand – frightened, happy, lustful, with pupils dilated and lips reddened – walks through the room, her hips swaying.

"That's her," the whisper goes around.

"They say she was Bonaparte's mistress!"

"That plans were afoot for them to escape together in a hot air balloon!"

"They say the last of her children, the boy Arthur, is not the Grand Marshal's child . . . ."

Dressed in black she appears sombre, but – inside, hidden! – she is crackling and impatient and desperate for change.

The thought of rubbing against people she has not met fills her with delight. She is shaking as she crosses the room, her eyes vivid and bright; eyes that say: *Now, I am ready for life!*

Her skirt brushes against an English officer's breeches as she walks by and she turns back, and offers her most winsome smile.

"I'm so sorry."

The man looks at her and his eyes move for a second – just a flicker – to the upper flesh of her breasts.

She turns away, sees their gate guard, Lieutenant Graham, across the room, greets him overloud, coquettes, hand on hip, against lip, eyes up and down.

"And how are you?" she asks suggestively.

"Busy, but well," he says.

"Busy?" she laughs. "On this island? It cannot be true!"

He tells her of his duties at the mess, and of all the things to be done before sailing in two days.

She lowers her voice intimately. "But would you not like to see the Emperor's rooms before you go?"

He looks at her in surprise. "Is it possible?"

"With me, yes."

She beckons him towards the door of the billiard room.

"The more I have seen of sovereigns," she says softly to him before they go in, "the more I prefer republics."

"Is it true what they say of her?" Bishop Warden asks Surgeon Henry.

"How am I to know? Rumour says so. But then what has there been on the island except gossip and slander?"

Warden nods. "There is a kind of soldier-like resolution in his manner, but I can perceive great sorrow in his heart."

"Who? Bertrand? Oh, yes."

"One expects to find Herculean figures in the service of the man who once bestrode Europe."

"Yes, I suppose so."

"And yet they all seem broken. A crushed Grand Marshal, an insipid Marquis, a bitter ex-Baron."

"Ummm."

"You saw him once, didn't you?"

"Not professionally."

"Is it true that he slept for most of his time on the island?"

"I don't know."

"He who once possessed sumptuous palaces in so many of the splendid cities of Europe, ending it here," Warden looks around, "in this pokey maze of a house, with a tarred canvas roof, and nothing to do."

"Madame Bertrand just told me that Bonaparte died of poison of the soul."

"And what do you think?"

"I don't know."

Henry and Warden stare as Madame Bertrand moves into the billiard room with Lieutenant Graham.

"They say the French are in great debt in Jamestown."

"The troops as well."

"One almost feels pity for him," Warden says. "Then one remembers that he wanted to make England a French island. Then one remembers."

"Ummm."

"Ahhh," says Warden, standing to attention. "The Governor's here at last."

"Marchand thinks he has laid out everything with great dignity," Countess Bertrand says, closing the door behind them. "He told me: '*If we are to exhibit the Emperor's possessions to strangers, they should inspire reverence and awe.*' But as you see," she gestures around the room, "it looks nothing better than a house sale."

"I would not say that," Lieutenant Graham says politely.

"There's a kind of order: maps and atlases, globe and compasses here; saddles, spurs and telescopes here; clothes here; books here; crockery here; and lastly items for his toilet."

"I am surprised in a way by how little there is. Did the Emperor not have any furniture?"

"Two garden chairs, his camp beds and a screen."

"And paintings? Jewels?"

Fanny Bertrand's face darkens. "Only six diamonds left on a string. The rest of his jewels are in Europe. I imagine that his crown is now broken up and sits on the necks of Bourbon ladies; ladies who - when they hear the Emperor's name - laugh and say, *Who? Who?*"

"I am sure that's not the case."

"Well, you know more about Europe than we do."

Lieutenant Graham looks through the piles of clothes - white cashmere vests, stockings and girdles - and runs his fingers over medicines, soap brushes and razors.

"Is the furniture as it was in his day?"

"Largely, yes. And look! Marchand has even laid out the last book he was reading."

She walks across the room and, in an irreverent half-mocking way, assumes the manner of a guide: "The Emperor sat here when he was dying with blankets over his freezing feet. On the table here is his coffee pot - observe the imperial crest - a carafe of orgeat and his calomel."

"I hope he did not take them at the same time," Lieutenant Graham says, grinning, "otherwise we should worry!"

"What do you mean?" she asks pleasantly.

"Not with arsenic in the same house!"

Something in his tone alarms her and she finds herself saying: "Of course not orgeat and calomel together."

"You have heard of the Brinvilliers case then, in France a few years ago?"

"We have not been allowed French newspapers here."

"I'm so sorry. Of course not."

She says vacantly: "Marchand tried to replicate this room because Sir Hudson and Lady Lowe expressed an interest in seeing it as it had been. We agreed at the time – we had so much to gain by being pleasant – but it has come to nothing."

"Your husband is very disappointed that the body cannot go back?"

"Very. He won't easily give it up."

Lieutenant Graham crosses the room and stands very close to her as she looks down upon the Emperor's death mask.

"Do you know, I think I will always remember his face now set like this."

Graham nods sympathetically. He starts to speak, hesitates, then starts again: "It is an indiscreet question, Countess, but why was it that Bonaparte did not honour you and your husband in the will."

She looks up at him coldly. "I don't know."

"I'm sorry, my question was presumptuous. I have upset you."

"Not at all," Fanny says more softly, looking into his kind green eyes. "You have done nothing wrong." She puts the mask down.

"Do you all resent the English very much?"

"We never blamed the common men. It was Hudson Lowe and the Government of England that we cannot forgive. Their petty tyrannies. Their disrespect."

She looks at the table again and sees the medicine bottles.

"What were you saying about this case in France?"

"The Brinvilliers case? It was quite the most sensational story of 1818! Or was it '17? Anyway, the case was this. A woman called Brinvilliers kept losing her male kin. Forgivable to lose one or two, you might say, but they were all dying. Over about twenty years – one by one – both the young men and the old became chronic invalids. Then, after a few years, they would all die suddenly after the visit of a respectable physician."

Fanny smiles politely, and runs a hand over the edge of the table.

"Everyone, of course, thought that there was some strange hereditary factor that was passed down the male line. But no-one knew what it was. In all the deaths, there were several things in common: the corpses were fat and hairless, and each invalid had drunk a purgative, specifically a dose of calomel, just before he died."

He pauses, then goes on: "It turns out that the Brinvilliers wench – let's call her Lucille, I can't remember her name – had been devilish clever. Her uncle was an apothecary and for two years or more she would slowly poison her male kin with very small amounts of arsenic. Never enough to kill them, just enough to destroy their good health, and so establish them in the eyes of the community as incurable invalids. Now, the clever part is this. One day there'd be a relapse, a doctor would be called, he'd prescribe calomel – well, don't they always! – the dose would be administered and washed down with some orgeat and bang! – in two hours – dead!"

Graham does not notice the look on Fanny Bertrand's face as she absently picks up a silver fork and asks: "Why?"

"You may indeed ask, why! Mercurial cyanide, dear lady, mercurial cyanide! This woman's uncle, as I said, was an apothecary and the Brinvilliers woman – Lucille – had made a few experiments of her own over the years while she was meant to be measuring out potions for him. The orgeat, which as you know contains bitter almonds, and the calomel, are both individually benign, but put them in the acid juices of the stomach and they combine to produce mercurial cyanide – a lightning blast through the stomach then – bang! – gone! Is it not devilish clever?"

"It is," Fanny says faintly. "It is clever."

"Oh! I can see I have upset you. How thoughtless. Please, Countess Bertrand, come and sit down."

"No really, I'm fine. I just have a slight chill, nothing more. How was she found out?"

"I shall tell you," Graham says with an immediate return to his bumptious and eager manner. "I shall tell you," he says again. "When they exhumed the corpses, they found them all intact!" He looks at her triumphantly.

"Intact?" she says flatly, putting a hand out to steady herself. "How so?"

"Arsenic is a preservative – well you should know that, Countess, your husband is a keen taxidermist is he not? So an arsenic body, although buried, will not rot."

Graham falters. "Countess Bertrand, I have really gone too far. How thoughtless of me, no really. What a wretched story to tell on such a day as this! I shall never forgive myself – please! – come and sit down."

Bertrand watches his wife – pale as moonlight – and the English officer – red and robust – come out of the room. It will not do to say anything. He supposes that their gate guard, looking so concerned, yet so pleased with himself, has pushed his flirtation further than she wished. He sees her walking through the room until she is drawn into conversation with another group.

"Don't you think so, Bertrand?" The Grand Marshal looks up to find Montholon, Gourgaud and Marchand standing before him.

"Pardon? I didn't catch that."

"Are you not wondering," Gourgaud asks, "why it is that March-and follows some of His Majesty's instructions to the letter, and takes such liberties with others?"

"What do you mean?"

"Did the Emperor not say he wished Marchand to become the guardian of his tomb?"

"Yes."

"Well, how can Marchand guard it if he's in France?" Gourgaud demands.

"He assumed his body would be in France," Marchand interjects.

"I am glad you can so confidently interpret the Emperor's wishes."

Marchand looks startled.

"I think that the Emperor probably said what he meant, don't you?" Montholon asks sarcastically. "He said 'guardian of my tomb' not 'my French tomb', knowing that it was possible that he might stay on the island, and so to include the possibility of either place. So, at least, I believe. What about you Gourgaud?"

"More importantly, what do *you* think, Marchand?" Gourgaud demands.

Marchand backs away. "I believe you are right," he stammers. "I have been . . . presumptuous," and, without thinking, he begins to feel for the cool diamonds, which for the first time this morning he fastened beneath his cravat.

Montholon nudges Gourgaud.

"Have you got it on now?" Gourgaud asks in a low, nasty voice. "Are you wearing that great necklace, like a little girl dressing up?"

Marchand snatches away his fingers and clasps them behind his back.

"You know whose necklace it really is,' says Gourgaud savagely. "It is Queen Hortense's. She only lent it to the Emperor when he was forced to flee. Now that he is dead, she will want it back."

"Oh don't, Gourgaud! He's gone quite pale."

"Let's see it, Marchand!" Gourgaud cries. "It's such a long time since I saw it on Hortense, and after all she was no great beauty." Then, with a speed of hand that surprises, he reaches up and snatches away the cravat. "Like diamonds on a chicken!" he laughs, before Marchand instinctively tries to cover his throat.

"Très agréable!" says Montholon appreciatively, as if to a young girl. "Ah, oui, bien, très bien."

Marchand does not wait to hear anymore, for he is running with all possible speed towards Pierron and the kitchen, with diamonds flashing in the light and great tears pouring down his face.

"Why are you always so cruel to Marchand?" Bertrand asks, turning to them with anger.

Gourgaud laughs and says nothing.

"We need to be firm with Marchand now," Montholon says. "If the Governor heard some of the things Marchand was saying, he might not let us leave."

"What is Marchand saying?" Bertrand asks, puzzled.

"I overheard him saying to Pierron that he will not forgive us for doctoring the Emperor's drinks."

"We didn't doctor them! It was our last resort. We were trying to save him!"

"We all know our reasons, Bertrand. But others may not understand."

"Marchand is saying that we hastened his demise," Gourgaud adds.

"That's ridiculous!"

"Of course it is. You must talk to him, Bertrand, before he goes too far. Otherwise I really think it better that he remains on the island."

"Perhaps there should be a decoy," says Gourgaud giggling, "something to distract Marchand. Perhaps I will challenge Hudson

Lowe to a duel! Or you should, Tristan!"

Montholon laughs and Bertrand says again: "That's ridiculous."

As he looks over their shoulders, he sees the arm of an English officer creeping around his wife's waist.

"Perhaps a duel is not such a foolish idea," Montholon says. "If Lowe continues to insult us, what's to lose? He's hardly likely to shoot me."

"You don't think he would kill you?"

"Hardly, Bertrand, when one knows his reputation as a shot. I doubt he'd kill me if we met at twenty paces, and that is far too close for the nature of the insult."

Gourgaud shakes his head. "You should not challenge him, Montholon, if it comes to it. It will look decidedly odd coming from you or I, when Bertrand has been the court's most senior man."

Bertrand is thinking of blood. Of how it will feel to have his heart opened. The deep sting of the bullet.

"Yes, that's true," Montholon agrees. "Bertrand, you had better challenge him. At sixty paces, and with a little padding, you'll be fine. And in all the furore no-one will remember what Marchand has said."

Gourgaud and Montholon laugh, and Bertrand says vaguely: "Yes. It's a good idea.'

Gourgaud glances at Montholon. "We are only joking, Henri-Gatien. We're not serious."

Bertrand looks into their startled faces and then back at his wife. "The future appals me," he says.

Fanny pushes her way through the house, and begins looking around the sheds and storerooms outside. *This badly planned es-*

tate, she thinks contemptuously, *this chaos of unconnected buildings; this unspeakable house, more corridors than chambers.* She searches through three or four outhouses until she finally hears low voices murmuring inside the wine cellar. She pushes open the door, and sees Marchand start.

Pierron clutches a hand to his chest: "Madame! You are quieter than a mouse!"

"Que faites-vous?" she asks angrily, moving towards them. "What are you throwing away?"

"The excess," he says. "We don't need our stores now."

"You're throwing away food?" she asks, looking at the boxes at their feet. "Don't we normally give it to the poor?"

"We thought the Emperor's things should be properly disposed of, Comtesse," Marchand explains. "So many things are being snatched up for relics. We shouldn't like the English to profit from the Emperor's death."

"I see," she turns very pale. "You are planning to destroy everything?"

They nod.

She begins looking through the boxes. "Open the wine, now," she commands imperiously. "Serve it to the English. The oranges and the bitter almonds, I shall keep." Then, as they look at her curiously, she adds: "You know what the water is like on ships."

"Comtesse, the Governor has warned us that there will not be much room on *The Camel*."

"The Governor can say what he likes, Pierron. Where is Arthur?"

"He is playing with the English officers, Comtesse. Showing them the Chinese pagoda and the Emperor's favourite hiding places."

"Bring him to me. That's enough playing for today."

"Of course, Comtesse." They bow and turn away, bewildered.

15

Countess Bertrand watches silently as their cases are carried out. Sitting in the window seat, looking out over the damp plains and touching the spot where the Emperor used to lean, she thinks: *This house never liked us; this house is glad we are going; it has conspired to throw us out.*

A memory comes to her. It is evening. 1818. The Emperor is not yet ill, and she is still eating at Longwood House. The light is fading as she enters the dining room to find everyone gathered and waiting for the Emperor. The same old faces: her husband, looking at his nails with that predictable look of despair; Montholon shuffling cards; Gourgaud pacing the room. The three of them turn to look as she enters. She sees their expressions in the fading grey light - at once hopeless, despairing, restless and jealous - looking at her not as they might if they came freshly upon her, but glancing up without any attempt to find solace, their faces bereft of amusement or flirtation. Just a raised eye and an ounce of hope quickly subdued, then a laboured greeting in a flat voice, "Bonsoir." This is the memory she will take with her. This is her St Helena.

She turns away from the wet window, and looks into the sitting room where Bertrand, with Arthur on his knee, is speaking quietly: "Do you remember the Christmas the Emperor gave you a drum, Arthur? And the time he bought you a billy-goat for learning your tables?"

"Oui, Papa."

"You must always remember how much the Emperor loved you, Arthur. How he used to call you his second son."

"Oui, Papa. Pouvons-nous aller maintenant? Can we go now?"

Negroes and Chinese move back and forth through the house. Fanny looks around from time to time, noticing not their faces, but the black and yellow of their hands as they pick up her boxes. She does not give orders because she no longer values anything here; because she would be happy for Bertrand's dead creatures to be poorly tied on and go hurtling down the mountains into the dark blue Atlantic.

Since she spoke to Lieutenant Graham yesterday, there have been a thousand thoughts in her mind. She has vacillated between telling and not telling. Last night at dinner she wanted to turn to each familiar face and scream: "Was it you, salaud? Was it you?" She has considered everyone from every angle: Who had access to the kitchens? Who had the chance? Montholon was in charge of the stores; Pierron cooked the food; Marchand carried dishes to table; and Bertrand, Gourgaud and herself have all, at times, served the Emperor coffee or poured him a glass of his special wine.

It would have been so easy to poison him, she sees this now: his peculiarly rapid eating habits, his predictable culinary tastes, his special dishes and wine. He once told her that he thought he must have escaped poisoning "not once but ten times," yet no one could have been more cavalier about precautions, and he had had no taster here.

Early this morning, when Antommarchi was taking his walk, she had stolen into his room and looked through his medical books. '*Les symptômes d'intoxication à l'arsenic,*' she had read, '*palpitations, headaches, extreme thirst, chills in the legs, loose teeth, pain in the liver, yellow skin, lack of fine body hair, layers of fat over the abdomen. On post-mortem examination: enlarged liver.*' Was arsenic, then, the 'climatic illness' of which the Emperor had complained for so long?

The simplest phrases are now complicated by suspicions. What did Montholon mean when he said last night that "the Emperor was predestined to die here"? What did Gourgaud mean when he said, "I am glad we have seen him through to his end"? Did the diamonds around Marchand's neck point the way to the truth? Or had Bertrand never forgiven Napoleon for asking that she become his mistress?

She hears Bertrand calling: "Fanny! All the luggage is tied on and covered. Come on. It's really starting to rain."

"Just a minute."

She hears Bertrand whispering to his son: "No more silliness now, Arthur. Not until we are alone in our cabin on the ship. Hortense! Henri! Allons-y!"

Then she hears Bertrand and the children walk through the house and pass out of the front door.

She asks herself for the hundredth time: why, if mercurial cyanide was responsible for the hole in his stomach, had Antommarchi not seen it? But then she sees that Antommarchi could have known nothing of the Brinvilliers case for none of them had read a French paper in six years. Then she wonders why the English surgeons did not suspect foul play. But soon that too becomes clear: Antommarchi falsified his account of Napoleon's illness, at the Emperor's own behest: "I shall not have my bitterest enemy know everything about me – my every symptom and evacuation and chill." She hears Graham's words again: "The victim is usually dispatched by a hand other than the murderer", and she remembers that it may have been her own husband who held the last glass to the Emperor's lips.

All the rooms are empty now, and this is her final chance. This is the time to run out shrieking: "Henri! Something terrible has happened! We must dig him up!"

But the thought of that big body rising belly-first into the air appals her; the thought of being forced to stay on for a day, a week, a month; to remain here to ask *who* and *why* and *for what*; to be forced to admit to themselves and to each other that ultimately they had all hated him, they had all wanted him dead...

She can hear someone beating a slave outside and wonders why, when people honour the dead, they can be so cruel to the living. A confession would destroy their lives, but would never bring back the Emperor. Surely they had all given him enough? Now perhaps, Napoleon just needed to serve his time underground.

The rain is pounding against the windows and the sky is dark grey. She walks through the empty rooms, pressing the palms of her hands against each wall and wonders: *What will happen to this house which knows all my secrets, which knows all the things I have thought and been?*

This is my last chance to speak, she thinks, opening the kitchen door, looking at the rain and picking up her umbrella. Then she runs – silently, and for the final time – from her six-year prison.

"Gourgaud! Montholon! Hurry up!" Bertrand shouts from the carriage as it draws up outside Longwood House. It is quite uncharacteristic of him to shout. Restraint and dignity have been his bywords here, so that now, hearing his loud cries, Fanny feels disturbed and asks herself if it is possible that Bertrand – dull, dutiful Bertrand – has all along wanted to leave just as much as she.

"Hurry up!"

Inside the house, the sound of Bertrand's raised voice unnerves Montholon too. When has he ever heard Bertrand shout in that unrestrained way, like a boy crying '*Come to the river!*' on a summer's day?

Montholon rubs his face and looks around. His room is almost empty. The fire is out. The windows are closed and the shutters fastened. Since dawn he has been checking the meagre furnishings of his room, his hand has gone *pat, pat, patting* into the corners of his cupboard, under his mattress, between the springs of his bed, feeling like a blind man into the dark nooks of his room. And with each examination he grows more frightened that some part of what he has thought and seen and known here will be left behind.

He knows he is being irrational, and he is not an irrational man, but he can't help casting his eyes once more around the room, patting the rough wood above the door, and sliding a finger into the tiny mouse hole near the fireplace.

He would - if he could - parcel up the air which knows his thoughts, and parcel up the walls which have watched him, and scatter them to the four corners of the earth. There is something altogether too solid about this house now, as if it were intent on holding something together, some definitive evidence of their past.

When they came back from the funeral, it was a surprise to wander through the house and find the Emperor no longer there. They had become accustomed to his body lying in state, dominating the centre of the house, just as they had grown accustomed to being commanded by his living spirit. But his absence after the funeral, Montholon now sees, was only a temporary illusion, for the house seems to contain more strongly than ever the spirit of the Emperor, and the spirit of what has been.

It would not be enough to pull down the house, to scatter the stones and allow the wind to lick them clean. The stones would still know. It needed a fire - fire was the only element that could eradicate what had been.

Bertrand's voice comes to him again from outside.

"Montholon! Gourgaud! Hurry Up!"

Gourgaud is overwrought. His packing is not yet finished. This morning, before dawn, he went into the garden and dug up rows and rows of plants. He does not know what to do with these plants, but he must have them. He must have them carried to his cabin on the ship and water them throughout the voyage.

He has broken off two shutters from the windows of the house, taken a shelf from the kitchen where the spices used to be kept, pressed flowers from their garden, as well as a butterfly that he found dead on the lawn. Now, bunches of willow branches that once overlooked the Emperor's grave are being thrust into his case. He takes these things not carefully or thoughtfully or with a clear idea of whether they will really survive, but manically, greedily, like a child attacking a bag of sweets. If he could pack up this house into a box he would do so. He would take everything, even the island, back to Europe, for how tiny it was after all! Just a few ropes around the edges and a few vast birds, and they could move it – the whole thing – to France, and people would come and pay their respects and walk through the rooms that had confined them and hear:

"*This is where Baron Gourgaud sat when he talked to Napoleon. This is Baron Gourgaud's bed.*"

Montholon's voice comes through his door.

"Are you ready Gaspard? Do you need a hand?"

"Non! C'est bon. You go. I'll just be a moment."

Marchand is sitting on the floor of his spartan attic room. He has rarely slept here; it has only been a place to keep his few possessions and to change his clothes. For almost six years he has reclined at night, wrapped in his capes, in front of the Emperor's door.

When will his duties come to an end? Marchand himself is not sure. He did not come to St Helena to follow generals, but, since Napoleon died, the generals have felt free to order him around. He has been asked to darn Montholon's stockings, to fetch water for Gourgaud's bath, and he has done these things because life has not yet taught him the luxury of refusal. In his angrier moments, he tells himself that he is no longer a servant, but a man with a diamond necklace, and a title waiting for him one day in France. But still . . . out of respect for the other servants, who have received so little, out of respect for Pierron, his oldest, greatest friend, he cannot refuse the servile duties, because to refuse them would be to say he has grown above them, the duties and the men; that he has become, in the end, one of the sofa sitters, one of *them*.

Since the Emperor's body has been removed, vacancy has filled the house and the wind has gusted through the poorly fitting doors, blowing away all meaning. Nothing has any importance now; nothing softens the blow. Napoleon's greatcoat, his britches, his bicorne and boots are all packed in Marchand's cases, but they are empty, lifeless things. A reminder of Napoleon, certainly, but nothing to do with his whole person: with the depths of his ever-changing grey eyes, with the radiance of his smile. For what is a bicorne without a brain to fill it? What power has a uniform when it merely lies there folded and flat? The man is the thing, not the symbol, not the parts. Events have made clear to Marchand that he is not a reliquist.

He hears the whinny of a horse and stands up, peering out through the tiny window at the rain blurring the pale green grass, obscuring the plains and the distant sea. Suddenly, there are footsteps running through the billiard room below – Gourgaud's, he knows from the light heel strike – then Bertrand shouting, "Come on! Let's go!" He can hear the horses being lashed. Where are they? The mist obscures everything. He can't see. Had the carriages been waiting by the green? "Wait!" he shouts, wrenching open the door and taking the outside stairs two at a time. He catches a glimpse through the mist of the carriages pulling away. "Wait!"

A hundred questions that he has ignored for days rise up at this moment like live voices. *Where will you go now? How will you live? What will you do?* The questions beat around his ears, drowning out the noise of the horses, the rain on the canvas roof.

He walks into the Emperor's tiny study, gazing after the shadowy shape of the carriages through the thick wet glass, through the misty white light, and his legs give way. He sits on the Emperor's chair, in front of the Emperor's desk. It's the first time he has ever sat there. "One needs to go to sleep on this island and not wake up for a year or two," he hears Napoleon say.

16

I watched my courtiers all the way on that slow drive to Jamestown. I sat beside the driver, looking back at their pale faces, and I
waited for Fanny to speak.

I did not know, of course. Not for certain. I never had. I had
only the suspicion that I was being poisoned, emanating from certain comments and looks, an elaborate insistence that I eat certain
'specially prepared' dishes, drink my 'special wine'. Then there was
that smile after my final glass of orgeat. A murderous pleasure?
Possibly. But the thought had also occurred to me – one that filled
me with a still deeper chill – that the smile might indicate nothing more than the simple pleasure of watching me die: nothing
murderous, or treasonable, just a satisfaction that I would soon be
gone. I was forty-six when I arrived, and might have lived twenty
years or more. Everyone wanted me dead in the end, so that they
could leave – the English *and* the French. I saw that now.

During that last month I had summoned my courtiers: "You
must continue with your duties," I had said, "so that I can continue
with mine. I shall go on drinking whatever you put before me, but
only if I have your assurance that you will follow my instructions.
Otherwise," I nodded significantly, "I shall start drinking the wine
that you drink." I looked up into their faces, but could read nothing there except sadness that a man who had once addressed kings
was now blathering like un fou. During that last month, the time

of my greatest bodily pains, perhaps I spoke to an assassin, perhaps I did not: I didn't speculate anymore, neither to work out if there was a murderer nor, if so, who he might be.

I justified it this way: everyone wanted me dead, and I wanted to be dead. Did I not therefore satisfy more than just my own soul? If I drank my wine rapidly, did I commit a crime? Why should God punish me for wanting to return to him a little sooner, for hurrying like a child to his side? Why should God – all benevolent, all forgiving – punish such an act? Punish me for choosing the French over the English, the quick over the slow? Punish me for helping my son?

As the horses began the descent towards Jamestown, clattering and stumbling on the precipitous hills, the Longwood party sat in the carriage behind me in silence, the children piled on their knees.

At last Fanny Bertrand cleared her throat and coughed a few times. But it was a minute or more before she finally said: "We know this island so little! If people ask about it in Europe, I shall not know what to say. All we will know is Longwood and Jamestown and an evening spent at Plantation House."

No-one responded.

"We know so little of the islanders," she went on, quietly, vaguely. "How is it that we have lived in such a small space – the size of Fontainebleau or less – and not known them?"

No-one answered.

"I just wish we might have met some," Fanny Bertrand said after another mile had passed. "They look such a clean, friendly people."

Gourgaud looked at her with a vicious expression: "The devil shat this island and its people as he flew from one world to the other."

He looked at the others, but they avoided his gaze, and no-one else said a thing. The carriage passed Plantation House and they all looked out of the windows, and that conversation - that shoddy threadbare conversation - was the only one spoken on the long journey down.

I tried to make myself felt, tried to remove the whip from the coach man's hand and crack it down on her head, but no matter how I tried, my hand could not grip the leather. Until the previous day I had still been able - with great will and concentration - to manipulate objects, but since my body had been buried, the last of my physical powers had left me. Now, all that was left of my material power was the discomfort that some people felt in my presence, a shifting nervousness, a restlessness in which they would move here and there, complaining of chills, complaining of heat, feeling - as my hands floated through their bodies - a sort of restless shiver. That, now, was all I could do.

A great wave of passivity swept over me then: a carelessness about consequences and conclusions. It was then I accepted that I could never know the truth, or communicate the things I had discovered.

As we reached the top of the town, the soldiers became more numerous and some of them seemed to recognise the carriage as it was passing, and saluted in a desultory sort of way. As we rumbled further down the main street, a whisper seemed to spread along it, and mothers drew their children to them, whispering: "Heads down! Don't look!" We rolled through the town, past the washer women and the shops stuffed with trinkets and baubles, past the neat rows of jacaranda, past the islanders in black, and finally through the drawbridge to the wharf where hundreds of red coats were lined up silently waiting. As they saluted - such respect, such respect - I wondered if a single person knew they might be saluting a murderer, the killer of a man whom 83 million people had once called emperor.

145

Finally we rumbled past the poor little kissing seat, and stopped before the endless sea, where Hudson Lowe was waiting.

"Welcome to Jamestown," he greeted my courtiers and handed Fanny out of the carriage. "The long boat is here to take us all out to the ship. We sail at six. But before that, Bertrand, please, a word."

He drew Bertrand to one side.

"We have found some letters in town," he announced.

"What sort of letters?"

"Gorrequer tells me they're in Bonaparte's hand."

"Stolen?"

"No, I believe not."

"What then?"

"Forgeries. But convincing ones . . . and with strong sentiments. Letters saying that his will has been forged, that he has been . . . betrayed by the French. A letter addressed to you too, Count Bertrand."

"Saying what?" Bertrand shook his head. "Where are they now?"

"In the Castle. Gorrequer has them. He's trying to find out who's written them." Lowe turned away to cough. "The forger has some odd intentions."

"What do you mean?"

"The letters are dated the 9th of May." Lowe laughed dryly. "They're written as if he were still alive."

Bertrand's face grew very pale.

"Don't worry yourself, Count, I have every intention of discovering the culprit before the ship sails. However," his voice grew softer, "the writing *is* very similar to Bonaparte's so we will have to assume that whoever forged them must have known his handwriting well." He paused. "I suppose, I don't have to spell it out? The perpetrator is almost certainly among my staff or yours."

"Where were they found?"

146

"At the Consulate Hotel. Have you any idea who can reproduce Bonaparte's hand?"

"The Emperor's handwriting was unique. No one could copy it."

I smiled as Hudson Lowe looked at him irritably. "I have already interrogated everyone on my staff. So perhaps you can think a little harder. Otherwise we will be forced to presume that Father Vignali has not been saying his prayers for the dead, and that the spectre of Bonaparte haunts us still."

Bertrand looked aghast. "Can I see them?"

"I'll ask Gorrequer to bring them out to the ship."

Lowe turned suddenly and grasped Bertrand's arm: "He was the greatest enemy of England and of myself also, but I forgive him." Then he released him and they walked towards the shoreline where the others were gathered, watching Gourgaud teach the children to skim stones.

At the clap of a hand, a giant negro came forward and picked up Arthur. Fanny cried out.

"Be calm, please, Countess," the Governor said. "The children will have to be carried out to the boat. The cutters cannot get closer because of the swell."

"Shall I carry you, my dear?" Bertrand asked.

"Why not leave it to a stronger man, Henri?" Gourgaud asked, indicating a nearby goliath.

"I can carry my own wife," Bertrand said with great dignity, and with only a small struggle he picked her up and quickly lifted her high into his arms so that she gave a wild cry. I will never forget the way that she – after the first surprised struggle – surrendered to his embrace, nor the way that he waded through the surf with the water up to his thighs, and deposited her in the boat with only the hems of her petticoat wet. I had never loved him so much as I did at that moment.

"The rest of us had better rope together," Lowe said. "The current is extremely strong."

In a slow procession, like a line of convicts, Gourgaud, Montholon, Lowe and his wife walked out into the sea, the foam splashing at times around their waists and the wind whipping the sea spray into their faces. Gourgaud was the first to jump into the boat and unfasten himself, but before he held out his hand to pull in the others, he threw something up into the afternoon light. It was a starfish, orange and gold.

"Our lucky star!" he cried laughing, "here at last!"

He thrust his hand over the side to pull in Montholon, and it was only then that I saw Tristan was shaking from his head to his boots and I remembered that he, like me, was terrified of the water. As I moved through the element that was not mine to join them, I saw floating on the dark blue surface of the water a dead bee, my sign, and beside it - full of life - a green fish opening and closing its mouth, as if trying to eat it.

I looked at those in the boat, all but Fanny and the children wet to the thighs. They sat rather stiffly, seemingly avoiding each other's eyes until Gourgaud unaccountably let out a laugh, and Lady Lowe began to chuckle, and soon the whole party was helpless with mirth: Gourgaud laughing wildly at the seaweed on Montholon's breeches, Arthur giggling as he pointed a trembling finger at his father's soaked trousers. There, in the middle of the bay, between land and deep ocean, the whole boat seemed to quiver with the laughter of those who still had life.

The *Camel* was not a ship of war, nor a ship accustomed to passengers, but a cargo vessel, disorderly and with an appearance of being badly run. Boxes and crates were lashed down haphazardly on deck with frayed ropes, and the barrels of water had been left open so that they were covered with a slimy green film.

Bertrand put his nose to a barrel and drew back.

"It smells as if it has been to India and back," he said to Fanny. "Thank goodness we have brought the oranges and the bitter almonds. Trust a woman to anticipate what the water would be like on board ship."

A man was moving around the deck, scenting the ship with vinegar, when the captain came over and introduced himself.

"There's not much space, I'm afraid," he said eyeing Countess Bertrand and Lady Lowe suspiciously. "We're not much used to passengers. It'll be a squeeze in the cabins, but we've nothing better. Everyone must settle in for the first night as best they can. Tomorrow we can juggle things around."

The captain disappeared and everyone stood on deck watching the last of the baggage being brought on board.

"Off then, my dear," said Lowe, turning to his wife. The two of them stood a little apart on the foredeck, leaning over the rail and watching their luggage being loaded below.

"To better things," she said, her eyes glowing with kindness.

He smiled at her. "What is the first thing you're going to do when we reach home?"

"I don't know . . . eat an ice on the quay at Portsmouth?!" she said, laughing gaily. "And you, my dear?"

"I shall write to King Louis and ask him to rescind the death sentence on Bertrand." Then, lowering his voice: "He still doesn't know about it."

"I thought you were going to tell him yesterday."

"He looked so broken, I couldn't bring myself to do it. There will be time enough for that on the voyage. And to draft my letter."

"Hudson," she said, touching his hand, "perhaps in the future there will be no need for letters. How many have you written here do you think?"

"Three or four thousand, I suppose. I shall have no-one to dictate to at home," he said, looking at Gorrequer who was shouting at a stevedore for handling their baggage too roughly. "You shall become my amanuensis."

"Me, my dear?" she giggled. "With writing that slants the wrong way, and who cannot blot my words without smudging? No, you will have some trusty fellow to do it, and we shall live in India and drink tea on immaculate lawns and watch polo in the afternoons, and no one will have heard of some petty European dictator, some Napoleon Bonaparte, because we shall live in their history, amongst legends and giants and names that are strange to us, as his would be to them."

"Gorrequer!" Lowe called out, as his aide reached the top of the gangplank. "What news of the letters found in town?" He beckoned him into a quiet corner.

"We have found the culprit, sir, a China man. We're not quite sure why he did it. Hoping to make money, I'd guess. He doesn't speak good English so it's hard to know for sure."

Lowe nodded. "You've burnt them."

"Yes, sir. It's being done now."

"Thank you, Gorrequer."

I watched my old jailor with fascination and disgust as he took his wife's arm and moved away, absentmindedly patting her hand as they promenaded along the deck of the ship. Despite their smiles and laughter, a dark cloud - made of pieces of rumour I had fabricated - hung over them and only I could see it. Only I knew that they weren't going to a rich new life in India - they were going to die poor, wretched and outcast. I felt no guilt for what I had done, for it had been a battle of reputations as deadly as any with cannon and gun. He had ruined my plans - through his directives about my body, the embalming, the gravestone, the letters - and I had ruined him. Lowe to me was nothing more than a fish that swims at the bottom of the sea, an insensate that may be caught and roasted without guilt.

Gourgaud and Montholon returned to the deck just in time to see a case of Lady Lowe's clothes fall into the sea, and to hear her let out a pealing laugh.

"She is either a halfwit or a sage, and I don't know which," Gourgaud said, shaking his head. "Still, at least she has some sort of *presence*. *His* stature is not at all imposing."

Lady Lowe, catching the words on the wind, turned around and laughed and laughed, and at the end of her laughter, looking straight at Gourgaud, she said: "He is taller than Napoleon and straighter than you."

They looked at each other for a moment until Gourgaud turned away.

The sails of the ships were unfurled, and the sailors were running back and forth on the deck, loosening a rope here, taking off some slack there. The light was becoming rich and golden, and it would not be long before the peace of dusk would begin to glow upon the world. On the wharf, the throng of St Helena stood waving handkerchiefs and emitting a low droning noise, and it suddenly occurred to me that, after the last of the troops had left, these few thousand island dwellers would be the sole stewards of St Helena.

The boats in the harbour were filling out their sails, when I heard Gourgaud say to Montholon: "Poor Bertrand. He told me this morning he thinks His Majesty may have been an egoist. *An egoist! Ha!* As if he's only just now realised it! I told him: We have done our duty and now we must disregard the rest. Napoleon was always cruel; that was his nature. And it is because of his cruelty that he had so many enemies and not a single friend. It is also the reason why none of the men who were with him on Elba, or any of his family, would accompany him here."

"He could be kind," Montholon said, looking at the blond-haired Arthur, "to children and servants."

"To inferiors, yes. Never to equals."

"Was there an equal?"

They laugh.

Gougaud sighed and shook his head again. "Poor Bertrand. He told me: 'There was no fortune for us here, no position. The only consolation we had was the consideration that Napoleon showed us. With the public snub of his will, I feel that the past has been poisoned.' That's what he said, Montholon: '*I feel the Emperor has now poisoned everything.*'"

"It was all hopeless in any case," Gourgaud continued. "I used to think that if I could just go on addressing him humbly, and spending hours talking about his lost battles, then I should eventually win his favour. Now I just wish I'd told him he'd become a fat and rather forgetful old man. I wonder what he would have done if I had said that?" Gourgaud started to laugh. "If I had said: '*Frankly, Your Majesty, your breath stinks, your hair is always greasy, and you can't see your feet for your belly.*'"

Gourgaud laughed harder.

"Or if I had said, 'Frankly, Your Majesty, you deserved to lose at Waterloo. You made the mistakes of an elementary school boy.' "

Montholon again said nothing.

"Or if . . . ."

"Don't, Gourgaud! Leave it there."

Gourgaud's face immediately lost its good humour. "Don't tell me how to behave."

"I'm not . . . it's just . . . if overheard, such talk would cancel out the honour of our last years. Napoleon was a condottiere, ambitious only for himself. We always knew that, Gourgaud. But if he meant so little to us . . . why did we do so much?"

"Because we hoped he would escape."

"He never intended to escape."

"What do you mean?"

"He knew he was destined to die on St Helena."

"How do *you* know what was ordained by fate?"

"I just do," Montholon said. "Or perhaps it is better to say that he made it his fate."

"So why did you come?"

"To help him in his final years. To record his decline and fall. To ease his passing . . . ."

"You frighten me when you say things like that. It makes you sound . . . sinister."

"I'm not being sinister," said Montholon, "just honest. What is a martyrdom without men to record it? How can there be a resurrection without a death?"

I looked around the boat and longed for an escape. I had to be away from the conversations, the crowds of people thronging about the deck, and, since it seemed that the only escape was up, I climbed the rigging.

From the mast I looked down on the sailors scurrying around the deck below. I examined my old companions, dressed in clothes that I had seen so often, and remembered the terrible voyage out here, walking on the decks at night and playing vingt-et-un and reversi in closed cabins for sixty-four days at sea. The thought of another two months closeted with those same men filled me with a crushing despair.

Was it possible for me to go back to France and expose what I knew? Was it possible without the letters I had so painfully written, with only the shoddy tools of a phantom's trade – ephemeral body and floating white sheet – to convince the world that one of my 'loyal and faithful' companions had been feeding me grains of arsenic all along? Who would believe that a royalist, masquerading as one of my men, had done with a few drinks what the armies of Europe had not been able to do with cannon and gun? Was it possible to explain that I, who had shouted for years that the English were killing me, had now changed my mind and thought it might be the French?

It had to be the English. It had to be Hudson Lowe, who had the appearance of an assassin, not my Bertrand, Montholon, Gourgaud, Marchand and Pierron, who looked like decent men. A resurrection needed a torturer, and Lowe had long been cast in that role. The sympathy for Jesus was because of Pilate, not Peter. Any other history would be my undoing.

An immense brown bird with golden eyes soared towards me, and began circling the mast. As its huge wings flapped about my head and its hooked bill and talons grew closer, I shouted: "Laissez-moi tranquille! Leave me alone! Take your acrobatics away." But it swooped around and around, coming back at me again and again . . . .

"Weigh anchor!" the captain shouted and the sailors with great groans began slowly pulling up the metal chain from the ocean bed. Once, I would have studied their method with interest; now I only noticed them with the emptiness of an old man watching a familiar trail of ants.

The passengers watched from the stern as the ship began to sail away from the island. The cliffs – which had dwarfed the ship – began rapidly to diminish and the island, at a distance, seemed to take on different living forms: to become a dragon with a scaly tail curled around its neck; then a camel looking to the east; then a humped oxen; until finally she looked simply like a girl dressed in green and brown lying on her side as if asleep. First she was coloured, then just grey and darkening grey, then, as we left her behind in the gloaming, she was just a tiny black rock in a vast, vast ocean.

"St Helena is sleeping," a voice from below seemed to say. "She is slumbering again. She's left in peace, finally, as she's always wanted to be."

I climbed further up the mast, to escape the voices. The sea was never my element: on it I felt nervous, as if my star was fading; I had never won on it, and I feared it, then as before. The sleek brown bird appeared again at my elbow, circling and cawing yee-ka-ka-ka-ka, this time with a blue-green fish in its hooked beak. I remembered the starfish Gourgaud had held up, and the dead bee. I saw the world spin beneath me, as if I were being carried into nothingness on the air.

Fragments of sentences floated up from below, mixing and re-combining: "*Nothing is so important as coming into the world at the right time . . . What a foolish thing you have been . . . ."* I looked around in astonishment, and the voices died away. I had the feeling that

155

I would outlast everything - all men, the earth, the sea. I took a hand from the mast and held it up towards the sky.

The rock was becoming indistinct. St Helena was now just a shadow amongst shadows. In a few minutes, the eye would have to strain to pick her out and shortly afterwards she would be swallowed by the black night.

As I held onto the island with my gaze, I thought how much like Corsica she was, the Corsica of long ago, before the Genoese and the French, before I was an adult, before the urge for conquest, and the fatal curiosity about what lay over the sea.

I had found the crown of France in the gutter, and picked it up on the point of my sword. Now - with as little apparent cause or warning - it was gone. I had believed at my autopsy that I had a moment of choice: to rejoin the body that had been torturing me, or to merge with the mysteries of the dead, and without a thought I had chosen to remain with the body that had given me such misery. But perhaps here was the real choice, the real fork of the path. I had begun my life on Corsica, ended it on St Helena, and between the two islands I had acquired and squandered an empire.

"I was born on an island," I murmured. "I escaped from Elba, the island of England was my nemesis and St Helena is my home."

"*Let go!*" a voice seemed to cry, the sails screamed in the wind, the brown bird dropped its fish onto the deck and then flapped away. The fish struggled for a while, thrashing from side to side, until finally it lay still.

I looked down at the ship, at the crates packed on deck, at Bertrand's bald patch and the little figures of Gourgaud and Montholon, and I looked again at St Helena. My family had deserted me, I had never had friends, my courtiers were sick of me. I was alone, without even the comfort of a faithful servant.

I took my other hand from the mast and, still holding on with my knees, gazed across the sea. Now the island was no more than a speck - but it was still so near that I could still smell her, and I felt the same longing as when I had first left Corsica. I thought with nostalgia of all the things I had only glimpsed: wild watercresses growing by rock pools, vast basalt columns towering into the sky, lemon trees. I knew that if I stayed there I could guard my body, and that my son would return to meet me there, because that is the duty a son owes his father. And, when he came to collect me, I would be waiting.

I put my hands to my sides, lifted up my head and rose like an arrow up into the air. I flew above the *Camel* until it was just a tiny dot, then I flipped and plunged downwards, shifting before I broke the sea's surface to glide above it. Then I raised my neck and headed up again. As I looked back at the *Camel*, ploughing northwards through the waves, I won't say a shiver of regret did not pass through me, a small hope that I might have a second chance. But then I looked forward at the island, and the voices began to chant and hum through the air: '*You are free* .... *You are free!*'

October 1840

17

The preparation for the voyage had been so long, and the weeks at sea so many, that when we first saw her through the mist of the early morning, it felt like dreaming. I stood on the bridge with the others and watched the smudge of grey at the horizon grow larger. I, of course, had never approached the island this way. But my father and the rest must have been thinking of the time, twenty five years ago, when they saw her for the first time, and she was to be their prison. We all felt the loss of the person who was missing – or rather the people. For my father, I was sure, was thinking as much of my mother as he was of the Emperor.

The wind was gusting first from the south and then from the east, forcing the ship to fetch about and delaying our arrival at Jamestown. But gradually, over many hours, the island became larger – became real – until at three o'clock a volley of gunfire sounded from the hills, and we hoisted, as a courtesy, the Union Jack and responded with our own salute. No sooner had our last sound dissolved, than the island responded with increased vigour from its battery on Ladder Hill, and a crowd of frigate birds startled by the great noise rose – as if in a body – and raised their own cries to the wind.

I looked with amazement at the sheer cliffs that rose from below the surface of the water to tower thousands of feet above us. The rock was what I most remembered: its colour and multi-colour. On a grey day it appeared to be the dullest brown, but now, with the afternoon light upon it, one could see the twisted beds of lava glowing orange and gold. It looked to my eye like a fairy's lair, though I doubt it appeared so to my companions.

"There's the town," my father said, pointing it out to me. "You can see the little church with its wind-cock in the shape of a fish."

"And look, Arthur!" Gourgaud cried. "If we were a little to the west, you would see straight up the valley to the heart-shaped waterfall."

They were finding their bearings, I suppose, and it was useful to have someone to whom they could address their observations. The bare land offered few landmarks. Only scattered huts broke the skyline, and a solitary tree bent and deformed by the wind.

"Is it strange to see again the place where you were born?" Montholon asked.

I nodded. "But the return must be stranger still for you." No-one replied.

The Captain, Prince François de Joinville, seemed as struck with wonder as the rest of us. He had not wished to take this commission for his father, King Louis-Philippe, fearing that his name would be linked forever with that of the man who had usurped the throne of his distant relatives. But he was a fine man, and had resigned himself on the voyage with good grace. Now he asked my father, respectfully: "And where is Longwood, Count Bertrand?"

"You cannot see it from here, but you see the furthest point to the east? That's Sugar Loaf Hill. If you follow the skyline southwards, you come to Longwood."

"Et cet endroit la? . . . the rock that looks like a man in profile?"

"It's called the Barn. Just a huge basalt rock. Home to nothing but a few goats."

Prince François nodded, but his gaze remained fixed upon the Barn. Even with my un-superstitious eye I could guess what he was

162

thinking, for indeed it did not look like the profile of an anonymous man: it looked like the profile of the Emperor. And I saw the Prince shudder.

"The island has a most sinister aspect," he concluded. "It's no place on which to be imprisoned."

There was an eerie quiet on board that was very different to the commotion we had heard when we made our anchor on the voyage out at Cadiz, at Madeira, at Bahia. Then, the sailors were full of good-humoured shouts as they went about their work, and a keen desire to get ashore. Now, crowded on the foredeck and the wings of the bridge, they looked on in silence.

I do not know how long we stood there watching. It was hardly surprising that my father and his old companions were mesmerised by the sight of St Helena, but what struck me later was how far we had all fallen into a trance. It was only when we saw the little island boats coming towards us that we roused ourselves and remembered our duty.

The crew had begun to man the gangways and the rest to assemble in orderly squares on deck, when Prince François led our party out from the bridge.

The wind had risen and the skiffs made their way towards us only slowly, rowing hard to move forward through the swell. Two small jacks flew from each mast: the pennant of St George and – below it, covered in tiny bees – the ensign of the Emperor. I was filled with gratitude that they should honour him like this, for I knew what a difference it would make to my father. He, however, hardly seemed to notice, and, when I took his arm, I felt a trembling deep inside him.

"Are you well, Father?"

163

He nodded his head.

"It must bring back so much," I said weakly.

"As it must for you."

"I feel as if I'm coming home."

He looked at me with astonishment. Then, without seeming to be aware of it, he withdrew his arm.

"Home? Surely it was never that."

"It was the first place I knew, Father. I suppose it was the first place I loved."

When I saw the expression in his eyes, I added: "You forget that I was a child, and that I never felt myself imprisoned. I knew nothing different. And it was such a landscape in which to play."

He looked at me again, but his eyes were far away, and I wished – as I felt the distance creep between us again – that I had not said so much.

"There they are," he said turning his eyes back to the approaching boats.

"Do you see," I said, "they have raised the Emperor's standard? It's a decent gesture, don't you think?"

Gourgaud, who must have overheard my remark, said roughly: "It's a decent gesture twenty years too late. Had the English been decent then, there would be no need for this now."

His son, Emmanuel, who shared his father's irascible temper, said: "Yes, Arthur, we should not pretend we have forgiven the English because such a little gesture comes so late."

A moment later the rope ladder was lowered and a minute afterwards the red and white plumes of the Governor's hat appeared. The feathers seemed to rise through the air very slowly, and it was only with great difficulty – and finally with the arm of his aide – that the Governor was able to clamber on deck. He looked exhausted from the effort, and it could not but be clear to all who looked upon him that he was very ill. His face was grey and soaked with sweat as he saluted limply, and asked breathlessly in a very English accent: "Le Capitaine du navire?"

Prince François stepped forward.

"Captain!" the Governor said slowly, this time in English. "*The Sunflower* brought us news of your expedition three months ago. Since then we have kept a constant watch. Only last week we mistook a corvette for *La Belle Poule* and wasted three volleys of welcome on them. It was Captain Jacquinot's *Zélée* returning from a voyage of exploration in the Southern Ocean." He gave a weak smile.

"We are honoured to have been awaited so decorously," Prince François replied, saluting briskly and gesturing toward the Emperor's ensign, which had been carried onto the deck.

"Yes," said the old man, "on an island such as this, we have little to wait for."

As he finished his sentence, a volley of coughs racked his body, and his face was quite purple before he recovered. At last he said weakly: "I am glad that you have arrived at last."

The Prince bowed his head. "May I introduce the men who shared the captivity?"

"Of course."

Prince François brought us forward and introduced us rapidly one by one: the generals – Bertrand, Montholon, Gourgaud; the sons – Emmanuel and myself; and the only servant – Pierron. We could see that the Governor was too weak for prolonged greetings, and I – for one – was grateful that salutes were not given, and that we were not therefore called upon to respond. For, although I knew my father would not disgrace me, I was not so certain of Gourgaud, or his son.

"We will prepare a banquet for you this evening," the Governor was saying, "and an entertainment for the sailors. How long are you staying?"

"We wish to return as soon as our task is over," Prince François answered. "There's trouble in the Peninsula and we don't wish to be held up in foreign waters with such a cargo on board. Besides, everything is in place at Les Invalides."

"Quite so, quite so," the Governor replied pleasantly. Then vaguely: "How things change."

"The soldiers who were once part of the Grand Armée would like to disinter the body. It would be their honour and his wish." He gestured to the deck where some of the Emperor's elderly soldiers were standing, or stooping, to attention.

"I had organised diggers, but, if you prefer, the Old Guard shall do it. I imagine you will want to see the island tomorrow? The house and the old haunts? Yes? And provision with water and meat? Very well. Then let the disinterment take place on Thursday, so that the body can be carried into Jamestown the following day. That way, you will be able to sail by Friday evening. How does that sound?"

"That sounds," said the prince, emphasising the sibilants in his unaccustomed use of English, "very good. Thank you."

"Very well, gentlemen. On Thursday, the 15th of October 1840, Napoleon's mortal remains will be handed over to you."

He gave a slow salute and was beginning to turn away, when my father said: "Do you have any news of Louis Marchand, Your Excellency?"

"The old valet?"

"Yes."

"He's at Longwood still, I understand."

"In the house?"

"The house is now part of a farm. The valet lives nearby. You should surprise him," the Governor said, laughing limply over his shoulder. "He probably doesn't even know up there that you have come back."

Then, with his back to us, the Governor gave a final wave and left.

That night the boats came back to collect us, and we stepped ashore for the first time. The town was just as we remembered it: the kissing seat, the little church, the wooden houses covered in peeling blue and pink plaster. A few goats eyed us from dusty paths scattered with succulents. Several ramparts still remained from the Emperor's day, several guns still pointed out from holes in the rocks, and there were old cannon balls - even now stacked in pyramids - rusting in the sea air.

When we reached the town gates, the drawbridge was lowered, and, as we crossed the moat, a line of English officers greeted us with shouts of "*Long Live the King!*" An officer stepped forward and introduced himself as Colonel Trelawney, apologised for the Governor being unwell and unable to join us, and showed us to the dining hall in the Castle.

It was a quiet dinner. In the absence of the island's chief man, the English officers seemed uncertain of the order of precedence and no one seemed able to assume the Governor's role. They smiled slightly and toasted us frequently, but no-one seemed sure what to say. They asked only perfunctory questions:

"Was the voyage good?"

"I trust the weather was fine?"

"Did you have fresh meat?"

And we told them about catching a shark off Finisterre, and the fresh turtles at Ascension Island. They listened and nodded with great seriousness, and then turned back to their beef.

Prince François had brought along the band of *La Belle Poule* to entertain the English officers, and they played quiet pieces with only the sound of our cutlery and chewing adding to the song.

We did not leave the dinner late. The sailors who had been feasting in the Consulate Hotel, at the top of the street, sounded as if they were having a far more jovial time. The noise of good-natured laughter broke the night air from time to time, interspersed with the tinkling of breaking glass and snatches of sea shanties.

We walked back to the harbour unescorted and in silence, each absorbed in our own thoughts. Mine turned to the vast cliffs, the huge night sky, and the distance we had come from France. The others, perhaps, were thinking of what tomorrow would bring.

The next morning, just after dawn, as we were waiting for the boats to come, I had time for a short conversation with my father, in which he made it clear that he could no longer look to me for comfort. I had tried to undo my words of the previous day - my feeling of coming home - and spoke instead of the fear I had felt being back on the island.

"You felt that, did you?" he asked, looking at me closely.

"I did. When we left the Castle, and the night was so quiet and still, and nothing was around us but ocean and sky, I felt that I might be left here by mistake and that, if that should happen, no-one would ever find me." I took his arm, perhaps with too childish a gesture of intimacy. "It is so far from France."

He nodded, and did not remove his arm.

"Did you feel fear when you arrived? For the first time I mean."

"It was like a nightmare, from which I have never fully awoken."

"Cher Papa!" I said. My voice came out very shrill, and I tried to lower it before I spoke again. "You should never have returned. I would have come in your place. I would not have wished your peace of mind disturbed for anything."

He looked at me with a grave expression, and said: "There's no possibility of tranquillity, Arthur. Haven't you understood that yet?"

Then the conversation was over and there was nothing more I could say.

How I longed for my mother at that moment. How I wished I had her lightness of touch! For only she would have been capable of cajoling him from desperation to laughter with one of her silly impressions or games. Perhaps I was too earnest, or too glum. Perhaps I loved him too much, or had too much of him in me. I wanted to comfort my father more than I had ever wanted anything, and I knew with absolute certainty that it was beyond me, and that I would never sooth away his sorrows or bring a joyful smile to his lips.

The boats were delayed and did not come until eight to take us ashore. This time the islanders were there to greet us. The word had gone around and, from the furthest parts of her mountains, the people had come. They behaved with exquisite feeling: there was not a single smile that wasn't tinged with sadness, or a single salute that was not full of feeling for all we had lost. These dear good people, who had guarded the emperor's body for near a quarter of a century, had come to pay their respects. And, though we were taking from them the source of their income, the bizarre attraction that had provided them with just enough for the last nineteen years, they still mourned for us, as we did for them. Had the English learned from their manners, none of this should ever have begun.

The road winding up to Longwood was lovelier than I remembered, studded as it was with brilliant colours and tropical blooms. Although my childhood memories were of playing in lush foliage in sunlight, I had heard so many stories from the men imprisoned with my father that I had begun to think of the island in their colours: dark and grey. Something of this contrast must have been on Prince François's mind, for he said: "It's not at all as I imagined it! From the sea it looks so bleak and barren, but the interior is wonderfully fecund."

For a time, even Gourgaud was happy to point out the riot of luscious flowers lining our way: "Look, cannas!" he cried, delighted. "Moon lilies and arums! Agapanthus! Everlastings!" But as we drew closer to Longwood, memories seemed to crowd out the colourful flowers, and only the Prince's expression continued to show interest without pain. On my father's face, memory after memory seemed to pass and leave its mark.

After some time, Gourgaud said: "Close your eyes, everybody! Close your eyes, and tell me what you see."

And, as if this was the most usual game in the world, squashed together in our carriage, we began to do so.

My father spoke first: "I can see Hudson Lowe coming towards me in a long cloak through the dripping rain. He is coming to interrogate me as if I were nothing more than a young corporal."

"Now he has come to see me!" Gourgaud cried. "He keeps calling the Emperor 'Bonaparte' and says that we need to discuss money matters: we are costing the English too much."

"He wants to cut our rations," Montholon said quietly. "We have been drinking too much wine and eating too much meat."

He sighed and opened his eyes, as did Gourgaud and my father. Only Pierron kept his eyes closed. His face was almost immobile as he said: "I can see the Emperor on his last outing, hunched over his saddle, his face pale and his features drawn. He rides as far as Black Sand Beach where the waves pound and pound. When he glances around, he sees the soldiers squatting on a hill, following his every movement with fieldglasses. He turns his horse around and says: 'Mon cher Marchand, this is the last outing I shall take.'"

After Pierron had spoken, the other men said nothing. I think, in truth, that Marchand's closeness to the Emperor still irritated them. Gourgaud did not approve of the riches he had been left, nor the fact that a man who had once been a mere valet would soon sit with them at a Prince's table. Pierron himself seemed to suspect nothing of this. He had travelled four thousand sea miles to bring his old friend Marchand back to France, and his thoughts were naturally all of him.

As we entered the rocky path that led to Longwood, we grew quiet. Montholon looked deathly pale, Gourgaud kept rubbing his head in an agitated fashion, while my father perfected the face I knew he employed most in times of stress: that of impassivity. So still was his face that I became afraid and wished that I had the seat beside him in the cramped carriage so that now I could at least have comforted him with the pressure of my body. Instead, I could only pat the hand of Gourgaud who had unashamedly begun to weep, and watch my father as he looked out of the window in silence.

We had been at sea for so many weeks, and had had so long to accustom ourselves to all that we should see, that perhaps we thought we could return with nothing more than a ruffle of our surface feathers. And so it was more shocking than I can tell, not only to witness the emotions on my companions' faces, but to feel what darted madly in my own breast. I alternated between anxiety for my father and a wild joy at seeing again the views that had lived so often in my dreams, and noting how the one differed from the other.

At last, we passed the two pillars where the sentries used to stand and, whilst all heads were craned forward for a first glimpse of Longwood House, my own eyes sought the house where I had been born, a hundred metres to the left. It was as I remembered, only more beautiful.

"There he is!" Pierron shouted.

"Who?"

"Marchand," said Pierron shaking his head at our stupidity. "Marchand!" he cried, and ignoring the order of precedence and the moving carriage, he wrenched open the door and threw himself out.

We saw the figure that Pierron had called to, turn and look back. Then, before our eyes, he fell to his knees and began to paw the ground as if he were intent on digging something up.

Pierron was instantly beside him, Marchand's head on his shoulder, and the two sat there on the damp earth for long minutes rocking in the eerie Longwood light.

How Pierron recognised him, I still do not know. I can only think that he saw his spirit rather than his outward person, for the figure in strange apparel before us was not the Marchand of my childhood. After long minutes, in which we were too nervous to approach, Pierron summoned us and, with his arm around his old friend's waist, beckoned us to follow him, seeming as if by some strange instinct to know the way to Marchand's house.

It was a long time before Marchand was ready to speak. He looked stupefied, as if in a dream, or as if he saw walking ghosts before him. In the silent minutes we sat waiting for him to recover - with Pierron rubbing his hands and patting his arms - we had time to take in the shoddy little hut, its banging shutter, the meagre possessions, and the old portrait of the Emperor on the wall.

After some time my father said: "We are so happy to see you, Marchand. This is the Prince de Joinville."

Marchand looked to Pierron for help.

"You didn't know we were here?" Pierron asked.

"I didn't think it could be true."

"You have lived here, my friend?"

"Yes."

"Why didn't you build a house?"

"I had no money."

"But the diamond necklace?"

"I have not been able to sell it. It's too costly an item for the sailors who pass by here."

"Then you have it still?"

"Yes."

Nothing will erase my memory of what then occurred: of March-
and moving through the gloomy dwelling to the rough-hewn sideboard and unwrapping a dirty piece of fabric. The light from the
diamonds illuminated the little room, and the brightness seemed
to eradicate – just for a moment – the smell of manure and poverty, and the sound of sheep baaing outside. Even the meagre fire
seemed to glow brighter for a moment, awed by that fine sight.

"You have had it all these years?" my father asked in wonder.

"I did not think you would be so long."

An accusation of sorts filled the little room. We had left him
here, abandoned and forgotten, just as we had been forgotten for
so long. But the six years of our shared exile had been only the
beginning of his, not even a quarter of the twenty-five years he had
lived here, his poverty increasing month by month.

"I wish I'd known you were coming," said Marchand gesturing
to his clothes. He wore a strange outfit, just a few pieces of cloth
tied in a certain way, and one could see from its sordid and threadbare appearance that it had served him for a long time.

"If you will wait outside for a moment, I will dress and show you
the house."

When he came out, he was attired in his old valet's uniform, and
it was a terrible sight. The years had thinned his upper body, face
and limbs, but expanded his belly so that the pressure of that flesh
pushed and bulged against the buttons of his jacket. Marchand,
who had been so slim, so sprightly and so smart, now had grey hair,
a paunch, and a grizzled grey beard on a face that had once been
smooth and bright. He shifted uncomfortably as we stared at him.
He had no mirror in his chamber, but perhaps our eyes told him
how he looked.

"You must prepare yourself," he told Pierron. "The house and
gardens are now part of Lufkin's farm. He's a rough man who
cares nothing for the past, and I've not been permitted to make
any restorations to the house. But he's not a bad man: he has let

me take other visitors around and he won't object, I think, to you having a look."

As we approached the garden, we saw the changes at once. The half-moon pond was emptied of orange and silver fish, and – with a half inch of stagnant brown water at its bottom – now provided a drinking trough for pigs. Half of the Chinese pagoda had collapsed and what remained had become a store for hay. The flowers and trees that the Emperor had planted were all gone, and the lawn had been destroyed by rootling animals. Only the faint indentation of the ha-ha reminded us of the ornamental paths that the Emperor had once laid out.

Inside, the deterioration was even worse. Nothing remained as it had been in the Emperor's day. A pile of broken spades and hoes stood in the middle of the billiard room, the dining room had become a granary and rusting farm equipment was stacked up in the Emperor's bedroom. The only thing that reminded us of the old days was the darkened patch of wallpaper in the dining room where the mirror had once been.

"If they wanted to eradicate all evidence of the Emperor," said Gourgaud angrily, "they had much better pull it down."

"I have often thought the insult was deliberate, but after so many years I see that it isn't. It is thoughtlessness alone," said Marchand, "that lets the past green into decay."

"These at least are deliberate," said my father pointing at some inscriptions on the wall.

"The visiting sailors leave them. They all walk up to see where His Majesty expired, and to leave their unwelcome gifts."

A hundred men or more must have scrawled their cruel remarks on the walls of the old dining room where we now stood.

One said: *Alive, the whole world. Dead, six feet of earth.*

Another: *Passer-by, do not bewail my fate,*
If I had lived, you would be dead.

Another: *Oh where and oh, where, is Napoleon gone?*
He is gone to St Helena, and his son has lost his throne!

"The fact the sailors wish to see this place is proof of his enduring legacy," Montholon said.

"Or boredom," countered Marchand. "What else is there for them to do when they are on the island for a week?"

Prince François appeared almost embarrassed. He had heard in the three months at sea so many accounts of our exile that he must have built an image of Longwood that was almost certainly different to this. A stunned silence overtook us all, until Marchand broke it by pouring out his recollections. He ostensibly addressed his remarks to the Prince, but really he seemed to be talking to himself.

"In the Emperor's time, small though it was, the house was well cared-for and surrounded by pretty gardens that gave it a certain charm."

The Prince nodded.

"The Emperor used to stand here for dictation in the afternoons," Marchand pointed to a spot nearby where two broken troughs now stood, "with his maps spread out on the table. His camp bed was here, and a second camp bed next door. He always liked to alternate the beds on which he slept. The chair he sat in when he was dying was here. And underneath it we would put pans of water to warm his feet, which were always cold."

"He used to like to face north," added my father.

"Yes, that's where he kept the bust of his son. On the table there was usually a lamp, his red madras headscarf, a glass and carafe. For many months, he would take only coffee or sometimes a little warm wine, but toward the end he began to prefer orgeat."

Montholon and Gourgaud coughed.

"In his last days and nights, we took turns sitting with him. Sometimes he would dictate to us for several hours, but often he was silent. He used to say of the wallpaper, which was green then, 'It's the walls that depress me, Marchand. They are the colour of suicide.'"

Marchand - lost in his memories - stopped talking, and we glanced at one another awkwardly. The Prince discretely moved away.

"I am going to look at my old room," Gourgaud said. "Come, Emmanuel. Let me show you where I used to live."

"Shall you see your old room, Montholon?"

"No." He shook his head firmly. "I'm afraid I will be overcome."

Marchand looked at him in sympathy. "It must be quite a shock. The changes for me have come slowly, but each inscription and degradation has been a drop of acid on my soul."

"Yes."

"And so this is the young Arthur Bertrand," Marchand said, seeming to notice me at last. "How grown you are - too old to be playing hide-a-seek in the gardens now."

I smiled.

"The Prince Imperial died," he went on randomly. It was both a question and a statement.

"Eight years ago, in Vienna. He was only twenty-one."

Marchand shook his head. "There are so few of his line left."

"That's the *end* of his direct line," my father said, looking at Marchand with curiosity. "His son was the last. That's why," he lowered his voice so the Prince would not hear, "the Bourbons and the new King of Orléans no longer fear his body being back in France."

"How wonderful that he can go home!"

"You too, you know."

Marchand didn't reply to this, but said: "I read your memoirs, Marquis Montholon. Yours too, Grand Marshall. Isn't it strange that we all remember such different things?"

"Do we?" said Montholon.

176

"I know some unpleasant things have been published as well. I haven't seen them," he added hastily. "One of the sailors who visited Longwood brought a book of anonymous cartoons, but I wouldn't look at them. And of course, those horrible letters are still displayed in town."

"Which letters?" my father asked.

"The forgeries. The ones written by the Chinaman, pretending to be the dead Emperor."

"But I thought they were destroyed when we left."

"You know how things happen here. The Governor asked that they be destroyed, but someone kept them as curios. Perhaps they thought they could make money out of them. Anyway, the Chinaman is dead now. He was in prison for years, always claiming his innocence."

"How strange."

"Yes, reading your memoirs I was amazed by our different recollections. I won't publish mine, of course, even if I go back. They are only the jottings of a servant."

I wanted to ask Marchand what he intended to do now and where he would go, but he looked so distressed standing there, that I dared not ask for fear of unmanning him.

When I had a moment alone with my father in the next room, I whispered: "Will he come back with us, do you think, Father?"

My father raised his shoulders and half-shook his head. "I fear he has lived too long in the past. He still believes himself chief valet of the Master of the World."

We did not stay in the little house for long. Gourgaud paced out his chamber, and called to us: "It *is* twelve square feet! When I told people that, I sometimes thought I must be exaggerating, but it really is that small."

Then we all moved in one impulse to the door.

"How did you bear it, Father?" I heard Emmanuel ask.

Gourgaud laughed as if embarrassed. "Sometimes I think I did not bear it well at all."

177

"Don't be hard on yourself, Gourgaud," my father said. "None of us were at our best."

"You're right, Bertrand. It was a trial. And we passed it. All of us. Just."

That night after dinner on the ship, when the weather was closing in and the wind shifting all round the compass, my father came to my cabin.

"Has Marchand agreed to come back?" I asked, standing aside for him to enter.

"Not yet. He'll stay on board with us tonight and perhaps Pierron will talk him round. But I haven't come about that."

He closed the door, moved into the cabin, sat on the bunk and said in a jovial tone: "Well, my boy, it's certainly been quite a day."

His demeanour was so unnatural, and his air of gaiety so forced that I became immediately anxious.

"Has anything happened, Father?"

"I hope not," he replied.

The little cabin seemed to fill with our silence, and I was just about to speak of the gale forecast for that night - the swells of which were already causing the ship to labour about - when he asked: "You have read my account of our days here, haven't you Arthur?"

"Of course, Father. It's very well written."

"And you have read Montholon's and Gourgaud's and even Pierron's diaries since they have been published."

"You know I have, Father."

"Then you know a great deal about the Emperor dying."

"Yes . . . I remember it, as well . . . though only, of course, as a child remembers."

178

My father smiled. "And was it not the young Arthur Bertrand who fainted on seeing the dead Emperor?"

I laughed. "I didn't recognise him, until someone called him by his name."

"Arthur," my father's tone changed, "there is something else I want you to read. Your mother found something just before we left the island. I would like you to bear in mind all that you know of the Emperor's last illness as you read it."

He put a book of newspaper cuttings beside me on the bunk.

"Start from the red marker."

"Where are you going?"

"I will come back in half an hour, when you have read it."

"Papa, you know how quickly I read. Please stay."

My father did not sit back beside me, but positioned himself three metres away, in the corner of the cabin by the door.

I opened the book at the red marker, where I saw my mother had written '*Le procédé de Madame Brinvilliers*' and began to read.

As I read, I felt the usual annoyance. This was so typically my father's way that I was immediately irritated. If there was something he wanted me to know, why couldn't he just tell me? Why did he always put a barrier between us, in this case the book? And for the first pages I thought as much of our estrangement as I did of what I was reading.

Whilst I read, I heard my father sighing and felt his eyes upon my face. I must have been thinking very slowly, because at first I could not understand what it all meant. The beating of the rain against the side of the ship and the pitching of the vessel disturbed me, as did those eyes of my father's, which I could feel examining me. I had craved his attention for so long that when I received it, as now, it seemed to paralyse me, whether with embarrassment or with pleasure I could not quite decide. I knew he was waiting for me to speak, but I did not feel in the mood for literary analysis, and the prose itself I found rather sensational, false and forced.

I finished the section he had marked, and said: "I am not sure what it all means, Father."

"You cannot see?"

"I don't see how it is connected with the Emperor."

There was a long pause in which he looked at me intently.

"You can't mean that he was poisoned," I said as the vessel pitched violently forward.

"I think that's exactly what it means."

"You should sit down," I said, moving up and making space for him on the bunk. "It's going to get rougher." But my father only moved his legs wider apart and steadied himself with a hand. I reached for my pipe and began filling it. "I don't understand," I said raising my voice against the rain and wind. "What do you mean, Maman discovered this?"

"The day before we left the island, when His Majesty had been buried for just one day, your mother had a chance conversation during which she heard of this obscure Brinvilliers case. Since she was so close to all that had happened, she saw immediately what you cannot. That the Emperor had been killed."

"Papa, how could he have?" And my voice, as I heard it, sounded indulgent, almost amused. "You said yourself that Sir Hudson Lowe had no access to Longwood. That he only saw Napoleon a few times."

"I am not thinking of Sir Hudson Lowe."

"The English officers, then. They were kept outside. They did not have access to the Emperor's food."

"You are right. Pierron cooked for the Emperor; Marchand carried the dishes to table; and Montholon, Gourgaud, your mother and I all sometimes served him coffee or poured him a glass of wine."

My father looked at me kindly. "Arthur, I have thought very seriously about telling you this. I don't want to destroy your happiness. And yet . . ." he passed his hand across his brow, "perhaps it is selfish of me, I don't know, but I need another witness tomorrow. God knows, I hope there will be nothing but bone."

"Father," I said, and I could hear my voice becoming agitated. "Don't speak in riddles. Explain what you mean!"

My father sighed heavily and began again, with that impassive face I knew so well: "You are right when you say the English could not have done it. They never had access to our food. Gourgaud, Montholon, Pierron, Marchand, your mother and I were the only ones who spent time in the kitchen. In short, excepting your dear mother, those of us who are on this ship."

"Maman? You?"

"I say it as a lawyer might. Of course we are blameless. But no one else can know that truth, as we know it, in our hearts."

I had to raise my voice against the wind in order to reply.

"You are suggesting that Montholon, Gourgaud, Marchand or Pierron *murdered* Napoleon?" I said, and my voice was very shrill.

"I can think of no-one else who had the means to do so. If you can, please tell me. It will bless me more than you would believe."

I lit the pipe and took some hurried draws. A feeling of unreasonable anger with my father overwhelmed me. That he should only now break this sensational news, speaking it in such calm phrases!

"I am sorry to keep repeating myself, Father, but I don't understand. If you believed this to be true, why have you not made the evidence public?"

"Because there is no evidence."

"Then are you sure you're not imagining it?"

"The proof will come tomorrow."

He looked at me.

"You have read the clippings too quickly, Arthur. Did you skip over the part that explained that the victim is usually dispatched by a hand other than the murderer . . . by medicines ordered by an innocent doctor?"

LOUISE HOOLE

"No," I said, though in truth I had not taken in the sense.

"It was Marchand and myself who gave the Emperor his last drinks."

The implications swarmed through my head, and I felt my face and neck grow very bright. I extinguished the tobacco, thinking that if I did not I would pass out.

"Arthur, you remember my birds?"

I nodded.

"How I found them on the island two decades ago and they are still preserved?"

I nodded limply again.

"Do you remember what I preserved them with?"

He looked at me, but I did not move.

"With arsenic. I preserved them with arsenic. It is the common preservative that all taxidermists use." He paused and took a deep breath. "If, when we see his body, it is still whole, we will know that he has been poisoned. If his death was natural, bone will be all that is left."

"Is this why you have come back?"

"Yes."

"Is this why you fought to have the Emperor's body returned to France?"

"Yes."

"Is this why you asked me to come?"

My father did not answer. And after a few seconds I began to cry.

I was surprised how bitterly I judged my parents in those moments as I sat on my bunk, with the ship tugging at her anchor, and my father by the door avoiding my eyes: bitter that my father was telling me only now; resentful that my mother had never told me. It was so typical of my father to be full of secrets more dramatic than one could ever imagine. And I felt in those moments how futile it had been to try to know or comfort him, or to understand the impulses of his heart.

182

Finally I said: "And you have known for nineteen years?"

"No," he shook his head. "Your mother kept it from me for ten years. She told me just before she died. She told me it was the weight of her suspicions that had killed her."

I started to cry again, loud rasping sobs, so that my father came close and put his hand gently on my shoulder.

"Arthur, please. Not so loud. The cabin walls are very thin. Tonight is not the time to yield to emotion. We can reveal nothing of our secret, either this evening or tomorrow. My reputation, your mother's, the reputation of our entire family is at stake."

I could not look at him as he stood there, his hand warm on my shoulder, and the ship pitching and tugging at her anchor. For the first time in my life, I wished my father was not with me, so that I could be alone to consider what I had lost: my childhood . . . that dreamlike landscape . . . my old heroes. Then the questions began, the endless questions that would send me half mad before the night was out. Had Marchand's deference all the time been a cover? Was Gourgaud's bluster a front? Was Montholon taciturn so that he would not speak the truth? And dear Pierron? Had I played in my innocent first years with a murderer?

When I thought back over my mother's life I could see - when I recalled certain looks - what she had known and never spoken of. I could see that this secret had divided her from my father, and I could see that this same secret had been a barrier these past nine years between my father and myself.

I felt the colour draining from my face. I looked down at my hands and they seemed lifeless and limp. The veins pulsing blue near the surface seemed at odds with the feeling I had of the life-force draining from my body. I asked my father to fetch me a brandy, and when he came back I asked: "Why do you need to know after so long?"

And he stroked my hair and said: "Because it is killing me not to know."

The next morning a frigate brought news that there had been a serious naval incident between England and France. The news instantly changed relations between the island and the ship, and all the previous practical difficulties of unearthing the Emperor's body came to seem as naught. At noon, the Governor's aide sent word that the old soldiers, who had travelled all the way from France, would not be allowed to undertake the disinterment; that the exhumation of 'Bonaparte's remains' would be led by the English; that they would be responsible for all 'operations' on St Helenian soil; and that the body would only become 'French property' after it was transferred to our outrigger boat.

Our party did not take the news well. It confirmed in our minds that the English were a barbarian and backhanded race. Gourgaud said: "A nation that insists its women sit aside after dinner is not to be relied upon in matters of decency and taste." And Montholon countered: "Gourgaud, you are just repeating what the Emperor used to say!"

Prince François's face wore a weary look, for as much as he detested undertaking this duty for his father the King, and his name being linked for perpetuity to the man who had tried to oust a branch of his own family from their throne, yet even more did he despise the English. Shortly after noon he sent a message to the Governor that he would not go ashore if he could not command proceedings. "Well I shall not be *subordonné à l'anglais*," said Gourgaud, and Montholon concluded: "Then let the English keep to the land and the French to the sea." My father shortly afterwards swore his allegiance to those who would stay on the ship, and Gourgaud's son, who shared his father's pride, declared that he would be "no *sous-fifre* to the enemy."

So it came to pass – after a day of negotiations and delays, with Gourgaud threatening what might happen if war broke out and shouting that we must at all costs get the body as soon as we could – that only Marchand, Pierron and I boarded the boat that called for us at nine that night, and it was only the three of us who were rowed by freed slaves, still bearing the scars of their shackles, towards the shore.

We did not arrive in Sane Valley until nearly midnight, and by then 'operations' – at the Prince's urgings, and with the Governor's consent – had already begun. The drizzle, which had brought a delicious coolness to the ship at bay, had grown heavier as we ascended the mountain, and, at the top, where we stopped, it was little less than a deluge accompanied by an icy wind. The English had set up two tents: one under which Marchand, Pierron and I sheltered, and the other as a chapel where the sappers could pray. I suppose the English thought this a good and proper Christian idea, but I did not see a single soldier stop and make use of it during that long night.

The light under which the sappers dug was poor. There was a full moon and she would have lit up the scene delightfully were it not for the heavy clouds and the rain. Lanterns had been placed beside the grave to supplement the solitary watch fire that spluttered in the rain, and the men were so much in need of light that there was only one lantern for the 'chapel' shelter and one other to cast its sickly yellow hue upon our tented night.

By the time we arrived, the bulbous plants that had covered the tomb had been dug up and placed to one side. Prince François had asked the previous afternoon if the sailors of *La Belle Poule* might be allowed to keep some of the plants, for he knew what it would mean to the men to return home with such a relic. But we dared not press the English on this, when the body was still so far from being in our hands. From time to time, an English officer would arrive on horseback and the senior men would huddle together for long minutes whispering. Each time this happened, I watched with anxiety until the whispering stopped.

As I stood beneath our shelter, I thought of my father's words in the tilting cabin the previous evening. He had said: "I felt the Emperor close to me for a long time. Sometimes I used to hear him calling out to me in the dark . . . but when his son died, I didn't hear him anymore. It was then that he finally left me."

I would have liked to think that the Emperor was about us that night, ready to talk, but as it was, I did not see or hear him. I don't believe, in any case, that he would have spoken to me when there were so many others around, for such is the way of spectres that they do not appear in public meetings or guild halls or in courts, but rather to those who are vulnerable and open and alone at night. Did Marchand think of the Emperor? Did Pierron? Perhaps not enough. For they say that thought alone can conjure up the spirits of the dead. Perhaps our minds were too preoccupied with practical matters – for we feared that the English might change their minds, or receive instructions to blockade or imprison us, or find a new way to withhold the dead body of the man who had played his part – more than his part – in this perpetual enmity between our countries, our endless war.

Haste does not rule a man in charge of a shovel. Only the nervous and watchful-waiting are capable of shows of great strength. The sappers went at the soil and then at the clay, first with shovels, then with picks, for hour after hour. We could not expect them to be Herculean, to understand our need for haste, but still the prosaic quality of their digging aggravated me, and it was only when I caught a closer glimpse of one of the men by the illumination of a lamp that I saw the disturbed expression of one who is not only exhausted but distressed by his work.

Marchand, Pierron and I said little enough during those hours in the lush, dripping valley. The exhumation of a body is not the time for fond reminiscence. And I could feel no pity for Marchand as he rung his hands and wept off and on through the night, nor find any sweetness in Pierron's backrubs, nor in the repeated 'Mon ami!' with which he sought to reassure his friend. Once the demonstration of their love would have touched me; now I found that my mind had disconnected the men who stood beside me in the tent from my childhood friends. The Marchand who had played vingt-et-un and marbles with me as a child, the Pierron who had fed me pieces of brains in the Longwood kitchen, those were men I loved, those were men I knew. But this pot-bellied figure with a waist-coat and a fob watch was not the same Marchand, and this Pierron with his skin hanging thinly from his bones, and his blue eyes glittering, white haired and whiskered, was not the Pierron that I loved.

Strangely, I did not find it difficult to erase from my mind the possibility that one of these two had been responsible for the Emperor's death. After my rage the previous night - when my father had had to restrain me from tearing down our companions' doors and demanding the truth - I had severed my understanding of what my father had said from any requirement to interpret events. I would do what he asked: I would see how the body had fared, and if it was preserved. But I would not once cast my mind upon a wider furrow than that. For I had determined, young as I was, that my life would not be glued forever to this sin.

If I was surprised by my own strength, it had yet come after a long night in which I wept for many hours, thinking mainly - I confess - not of the Emperor but of my mother. And the howling wind and the tugging of the anchor against its chain seemed perfectly to frame my mood of desperation. Now the damp mist seemed to confirm that the mind must close down, not open up, if it is to survive; and that by annihilating the questions - the *what ifs*, the *hows*, the *whys*? – it would perhaps be possible to live on with this unwelcome secret, as my father had done.

By three o'clock the men had leveraged up the immense Portland flagstones and were slowly chiselling away at the Roman cement immediately above the coffin. I thought of his body lying inside the earth – perhaps still flesh, perhaps just bone – and it seemed impossible that he would not be awoken by the unaccustomed noise, or that his spirit would not be roused by knowing he would soon be on his way home again, to rest among the French people whom he swore to have loved so much. I wondered a second time if we would feel his spirit about us, awakened by the flurry, but I, at least, did not. I suppose events were not, in fact, at all as the Emperor had intended. He had imagined a revolution, inspired by his body and led by his son, yet his dynasty had expired years ago. His poor son, Napoleon II, never crowned, and buried at twenty-one. Imprisoned, so it was said, by his Austrian relatives, never knowing who his father had been, never mind ruling France in his name. What a waste, I thought. What a crazy gamble and a waste. Then feeling my distress rising, I shut down all thought.

"Are you cold?" Marchand asked, raising me from my reveries.

"No."

"Please," he said shivering beside me, "I'm used to the climate. Take my coat."

"Non merci," I said, turning away, but he caught my hands and began examining them.

"Your hands are so small!" he exclaimed. "They are just like his. You have your father's hands." Then he smiled, released me and said, "The Emperor was so fond of you, Arthur. Try not to forget that."

I said nothing, thinking only that my hands had always been likened to my mother's.

"There is so much that I could tell you, Arthur. So much."

Pierron shook his head. "It's all in the past, mon cher Marchand," he said. "It's all in the past."

When dawn came, they had still not cracked through the Roman cement. The men were given a break and served hot soup. With the first light, sea birds came swooping and chattering, gannets and terns and boobies looked down upon us, calling and crying. Perhaps it was the unexpected turbulence in the quiet valley that attracted them, or perhaps – the thought came to me with a shiver of fear – they could already smell the aroma of dead meat. The birds kept up a continual call: *It is raining today in Longwood Bay* they seemed to shriek. Then they changed their cry: *Napoleon is leaving us.* Everything was white and green and grey.

The rain was still falling, when finally – at seven in the morning – the first shovel hit the top of something wooden, and the eyes of the men seemed all at once to round like moons, and their hands to begin digging with renewed vigour. As the top of the mahogany coffin came into view, the Abbé began to chant *De Profundis*, and the choir boys sang with him, their high ethereal voices soaring horridly over his baritone. I believe that everyone in the valley hoped Colonel Trelawney would tell them to stop.

The English officers were in the chapel tent changing into clean uniforms when Dr Guillard arrived.

"I've been sent by the Governor," he said to anyone who would listen, introducing himself and shaking hands at random, though he did not say for what purpose he had come. Perhaps the Governor feared that Napoleon was still alive? Or perhaps he wished him certified still and everlastingly dead? But for certain it seemed a strange thing to send for a doctor, when the need for one had so long passed.

Now, at the unearthing of the outer mahogany envelope, the doctor was called upon to confirm that a small corner of the coffin had rotted, presumably from moisture emanating from the stream that ran but a few metres to the east, and from which the Emperor had once received his drinking water. Doctor Guillard's face seemed to acknowledge his curious role, called upon to diagnose the humours of a coffin.

"Much too much moisture in this corner," he said with a wry grimace. "The north-west corner of the mahogany is rotten right through."

The officers nodded with great seriousness, as if they themselves could not have recognised such a thing, and I believe that someone even wrote down his words.

The order went up to remove the lid and sides of the outer wooden coffin, whilst the rest of the sarcophagus was still in the ground, for they feared that the wood would be too fragile to support the interior weight. Then the sappers erected a pulley, and began the exhausting effort of lifting the lead coffin from the ground. With an audible groan the coffin came apart from the earth and then, with creaks and cries and grunts, rose inch by inch into the air. It hung there, for endless minutes, the lead slicked by rain, a black jewel suspended in the St Helena sky.

The Governor, who had been kept informed of events during the night via a runner, arrived just as they had swung the leaden coffin onto the ground and were beginning to saw through the silver nails. As we began to crowd around, Marchand reminded me that there were two more casings to remove before we would uncover the body. I do not remember anyone talking in these last minutes except the officers who gave their orders in short phrases: *Steady . . . Careful . . . That's it!*

Finally there was only one lid between whatever remained of the Emperor and our eyes. And it was Dr Guillard who, with some agitation, grasped the edge of the lid and swung it down onto the ground. In that moment no one spoke. The only sound was the laboured breathing of the Governor, and the gasps that came – despite my best intentions – from my own mouth.

At first, all that could be made out was a recumbent effigy covered by a white satin shroud. After a few seconds, I realised that the satin was not a shroud, but the upper lining of the coffin, which had dropped from the lid where once – nearly twenty years ago – it must have been pinned.

Dr Guillard began. He, like all doctors, must have seen some dreadful sights, but he rose to the occasion and with steady hands began to roll up the white satin, starting from the feet. He rolled from the sole to the top of the boot, past the caskets squeezed between the Emperor's calves, past the silver dishes containing his stomach and his heart, past the bicorne hat resting on his knees, up past the sword of Marengo, the silver fork, knife and spoon, the silver plate and sauce dish, past the green belt of the cape of Marengo and the scatterings of coins, past the hands that appeared most horribly alive, until finally – with one further turn of the cloth – we saw the Emperor's face.

How to describe those moments, the emotions that rushed through my heart, or the intensity of the pulses that beat in my ears? Time seemed to elongate so that every new inch uncovered seemed to take an hour. And whilst a weak voice in my head had already begun to whisper *Murder* – to sound the word again and again – another part of me, the animal part, my stomach, was rebelling at the sight. The Emperor was almost exactly as I remembered him, except that a greyish layer of mould covered the features of his face. It was true that the cheeks were swollen, the bridge of the nose had given way, and the orbs of the eyes had hollowed, but, despite these changes, his swollen lips were half-opened as if mid-way through a speech, and he still had a few eyelashes on his lids. A bluish-grey beard showed on what must once have been a freshly-razored chin, and even his hair – which had been shaved for the death mask – had grown underground and was now several inches long.

He seemed both alive and dead in equal measures: the abdomen unnaturally concave, yet the hands so appallingly alive you felt they might at any moment wag an amused finger or reach out and pat a head.

"Do you recognise him?" Dr Guillard asked in a terrible voice.

"It is him," Pierron said, shaking his head in wonder, "Only more like he was in life, than when he first died."

Marchand did not speak. I think he could hardly believe that his old hero and friend still existed in some recognisable form; that he was not now, after near twenty years in the ground, mere shreds of clothing and a neat pile of bones.

Dr Guillard touched his eyelids and declared them "hardened," the hands when he brushed them were unyielding "like those of a mummy," the limbs had "shrunken in size," but the skin, he said, "retained a colour usually only seen in life."

With his medical report complete, the doctor scratched away at the mould covering the imperial boots. Then his eyes grew large and fixed as he realised that one of them had split, and that from the hole four toes protruded, each with a long yellow nail.

"Two minutes," someone cried, indicating that the coffin should now be closed. For what is air, but an eroder of flesh, and what is oxygen but a corroder of death?

"I cannot risk removing the heart or the stomach," said Dr Guillard, "for I fear they have adhered to his thighs."

The *Croix des Braves*, the engravings on his epaulettes, and his Iron Cross glimmered for a moment, and the vessels carrying his organs flashed their darkened silver. Then Dr Guillard sprinkled preservative saltpetre over the body, covered the corpse with white satin, and the Emperor disappeared for the final time from the eyes of the living.

Everything from this point seemed to take place in the unreality of a dream. I observed only distantly the body, packed inside the tin, oak and lead coffins of 1821, placed inside the triplicated sarcophagus we had brought from France. Someone said, "There will be many layers of protection now against weather and time." The outer casing was locked and the vast gold key was handed to me.

Eight English soldiers transferred the coffin onto a reinforced hearse, and we began to follow it through the twists and turns of the island in silence. The Abbé and his choirboys led the procession, the English soldiers brought up the rear, while Marchand, Pierron, Dr Guillard and I walked beside the coffin, each carrying a corner of the purple funeral pall, embroidered with a vast gold N. It was an arduous journey, made harder still by the growing heat of the day, and the heavy sarcophagus that had been built in France without a thought for the island's mountainous terrain. At the summit of each hill, the horses that drew the hearse had to be unleashed, and twenty men or more had to walk in front of it, using their shoulders to prevent the coffin hurtling down the hill. At the bottom, the horses were leashed again, and the men moved to the back to help push. I saw it and didn't see it. It took place around me, but didn't touch me; it entered my eyes, but not my heart. A funeral gun blasted out at minute intervals, and it was only this, punctuating the many hours of our laborious journey back to the ship, which seemed to shake me for a few seconds every minute from my trance.

It was late in the afternoon when we arrived in town, wretched with fatigue and heat. Father Vignali had come ashore to join the English Abbé in saying the Prayers of Commendation for the Dead, and when they had finished, the choirboys started to chant – an eerie, echoing, high-pitched sound that seemed to frighten away even the goats. A wharf-side crane creakily lifted the weighty burden as the choristers sung, and we watched as a dozen men, with great difficulty, manoeuvred the swinging coffin from the hearse to the waiting boat. I wondered whether the horses which had pulled the hearse, or the men who had thrown their shoulders behind or in front of the coffin would ever be the same again, and in those moments I felt it would be too much for any other creature to be maimed for the Emperor's will.

They had reinforced the hearse but they could not reinforce the long boat and the sarcophagus was so heavy – and lay so low in the water – that only myself, Father Vignali and six rowers were able to clamber aboard.

The sun was setting over the Atlantic and the funeral guns, which had begun when we left Sane Valley, still pounded out every minute. The air was thick with gunpowder and the cries of disturbed birds, which sounded to me then like the cries of men injured in battle. In between each blast of cannon everything was quiet: just the distant chants of the choirboys and the murmurs of Father Vignali beside me reading the prayers of intercession by the light of the lamp at the bow.

I glanced back at the shore and saw Marchand waiting for the next boat, with Pierron's cape around his shoulders and his old friend's arm around his waist. Then I watched the rowers and saw the sweat on their arms – backlit suddenly by the setting sun – turn blood red. As we drew closer to *La Belle Poule*, I looked forward for the first time and saw the old soldiers silhouetted on deck peering out impatiently for their first glimpse of their Emperor's body. I searched among them for my father's face but nothing could be clearly distinguished in the gloaming.

I knew that I had the answer my father had been looking for, but I did not know what the news would do to him, nor how I should be able to speak of it. Yet, for all the love in the world, I could not conceal the truth, which so many men had seen.

As I rehearsed my speech to him, I remembered a little ditty from my childhood that my old nanny used to sing: "There's nothing that keeps its youth so far as I know but a tree and Truth." And I remembered how on that long walk down to Jamestown, one of the English soldiers, believing himself downwind of us, had whispered to his companion: "They say that only the Egyptians can preserve a body so."

Perhaps I could tell my father that this was Egypt's final gift to the emperor, a mysterious gift from the country he had so loved. Perhaps I could point out that none of his St Helena birds and insects, preserved with arsenic, had survived with the Emperor's freshness of look.

At that moment, as I gazed westward toward the sun, the shape of Napoleon appeared, his hands stretched out in entreaty, his intense grey eyes burning into mine, as if there were something essential – something about destiny – that he needed to tell me. But a moment later, a commotion broke out on the ship. Thinking I heard my father cry out, I instinctively jerked my head to look. When I turned back, the form had begun dissolving, dispersing into the island air.

LOUISE HOOLE

Notes for Historians

Every day I cast off a little more of my tyrant's skin.

- Napoleon reflecting on the impact of his imprisonment on St Helena, as quoted in Kauffman's *The Dark Room at Longwood*.

Napoleon was exiled to St Helena in 1815. The men and women who accompanied him there left an exceptionally detailed record of their time on the island in the form of letters, diaries and memoirs. If you were to read this entire archive, you could pretty much discover everything that Napoleon did, said, wore and ate during the last six years of his life. What he thought, however, would be far harder to fathom, for although he spent his days dictating what was intended to become a grand public history of his former free life, Napoleon was one of the few exiles who didn't leave an intimate account of his days as a prisoner at Longwood. He had thought of himself in his youth as "surrounded by men, but always alone." On St Helena, he was truly so. As time passed, he increasingly isolated himself not only from the life of the island but from his own courtiers, spending hours alone meditating on past mistakes in his small bathtub. *Black Rock* grew out of a fascination with the millions of words left from this period: with the garrulous verbosity and the silences, of what came to be recorded and what exists between the lines.

In turning the events of Napoleon's 'last phase' into historical fiction, I have drawn closely on primary source material, yet at the same time taken liberties with it. The following paragraphs are written for those who like to know what is real and what is made up. Readers who don't want to fracture the fictional world of the novel can put down the book now.

All the key characters of *Black Rock* (the Bertrands, the Lowes, the Montholons, Gourgaud, Marchand and Antommarchi) are based on real people, all of whom left some account of the exile they shared with Napoleon. Some records (such as the thousands of letters written by the Governor, and stored in the British Library as 'The Lowe Papers') are so vast that they have not yet been fully examined, and may still hold surprises for future historians. Others are single slender volumes or condensed memoirs. Bertrand's exceptional diary, fuelled by the paranoia and lack of privacy at Longwood, was written in a code so complex that it was not cracked and made public until 1949, a staggering 128 years after the events described. Accounts like Marchand's were published later still, in his case posthumously and against his express wishes.

First-hand accounts were, therefore, my starting points for understanding the characters of the aristocrats, soldiers and servants who shared the claustrophobic life of Longwood House. I drew particularly on Montholon's *Histoire* (1846) and *Récits* (1847), Gourgaud's *Journal* (1899), Bertrand's *Cahiers* (1949), and Marchand's *Mémoires* (1955). The primary characters are, if you like, 'true' or 'real': for I have tried to portray their struggles, arguments and passions to the full extent of my ability, understanding and position in time and history (as well, of course, as their capacity to fit into the frame of my story).

Important information from St Helena during this period is also gleaned in the works of O'Meara's *Voice* (1819), Dr Arnott's *Account* (1822), Las Cases's *Mémorial* (1823), Arthur Bertrand's *Lettres* (1841), Dr Henry's *Events* (1943), Dr Antommarchi's *Mémoires* (1825), Albine de Montholon's *Souvenirs* (1901) and Louis Saint-

Denis's *Souvenirs* (2000). It is interesting to note how long after the events described so many of the first hand accounts were published, and how many remain unpublished (for example, a mass of papers by Napoleon's shrewdly observant scribe and librarian, Saint-Denis).

The secondary source material is too immense to mention in detail here. Napoleon is, after all, one of the most written-about figures in history. Most of his biographers find it impossible not to take a position on him, and, in the end, one accepts – and even begins to relish – their lack of objectivity. I particularly enjoyed Frank McLynn's *Napoleon* (1997), Lord Rosebery's *The Last Stage* (1900), Jean-Paul Kauffman's *The Dark Room at Longwood* (2000), as well as the wonderful novel by Simon Leys, *The Death of Napoleon* (1991). Jean Tulard and Gilbert Martineau have also written remarkably vivid histories of his time on St Helena. I drew heavily on Martineau's *Napoleon's Last Journey* (1976) for the events of 1840. For the sound of Napoleon's distinctive voice, it's worth reading some of his letters, accessible in various published collections.

Historians of the St Helena period will know that one of the characters in the novel, Baron Gaspard Gourgaud, was no longer on the island when Napoleon died: he had left under a cloud in early 1818, having accused the Emperor of having an affair with Albine de Montholon. I chose to include him in 'the final few' because I was fascinated by his passion; because he was that rare sort of man who shouts his truth, rather than demurs, even when speaking to emperors. Without his account, the Longwood archive would be far less colourful.

For simplicity's sake, some major characters of the latter part of the exile do not feature in my story (his coachman, Achille Archambault, for example, and his second and third valets, St Denis and Noverrez). A few major characters from the earlier part of the exile, including Las Cases (Napoleon's main secretary and chosen companion), Cipriani (his Corsican maître d'hôtel and spy), Santini (his Corsican usher), Joseph Archambault (his groom), Dr Barry O'Meara (his Irish doctor) and Marquise Albine de Montholon (alleged to have become Napoleon's mistress on the island) are also not part of my *dramatis personae*. All of the latter played important roles in the exile, but had died or left the island by the end of July 1819.

Aside from the 'cast', early readers have wanted to know about a number of other historical details. To answer their main questions in brief: yes, Napoleon was really exhumed in 1840, almost 20 years after he had died, and found to be whole and preserved; yes, the Brinvilliers poisoning was a real case (though some non-medical details have been changed for the novel); and yes, Napoleon's son died of tuberculosis as a young man of 21, knowing almost nothing about his father, and having been kept a virtual prisoner in the palaces of his maternal family in Austria. Napoleon *did* allegedly proposition Madame Bertrand; there were rumours that Arthur was Napoleon's child; but also that Napoleon had an affair with Montholon's wife, Albine (who left in July 1819 and is only alluded to in my story). It is also true that Napoleon left a diamond necklace valued at one million francs to his valet, Marchand; that there were many fantastical plans hatched for his escape (including whisking him away in a hot air balloon or in a primitive submarine); and that Hudson Lowe did indeed die in penury with his reputation in tatters: the mud that Napoleon had quite calculatingly slung at his jailor had stuck.

Despite all this verisimilitude, *Black Rock* is a novel, a fictionalised and playful account in which creative liberties are taken with past events. The truth gets distorted in historical novels: rooms become repainted in different colours; portraits on the walls get swapped around; fires get stoked or extinguished; people meet who never met. Most changes are made to simplify, focus, speed up or slow down events, or to illustrate a larger, different or difficult aspect of the historical truth. So, for example, the size and layout of the rooms of Longwood House were not in reality quite how they are portrayed in my novel; Hudson Lowe saw Napoleon five or six times, not three; Dr Antommarchi actually led the post-mortem examination (not my fictional Chapman), though there were the same number of British doctors in attendance (seven); Napoleon's body was washed and laid out two hours after the autopsy (not the following morning, as happens in *Black Rock*); the French had more information about Europe than I allow them, through a network of informers (though they were officially forbidden to read the papers or receive news). I should specify that the letters and diaries quoted in the novel are not translations of actual documents, but created from my own imagination.

There is also no evidence that a dinner, like the one I describe in chapter 8, took place in 1821, but the atmosphere of increased cordiality between the jailor and his former prisoners is accurate and real, as are the types of foods that Lowe, as Governor, might have served at the feast. Although the amounts of money bequeathed to the main characters are largely accurate, Gourgaud was, in truth, left nothing. Jacob's Ladder (such a distinctive part of Jamestown today) wasn't actually built until 1828, although in *Black Rock* Napoleon stands at the top of it 1821, and it was Madame Bertrand who actually said, "The devil shat this island as he flew from one world to another," not an angry Gourgaud. In the novel, the French leave from the beach, wading out through the sea to board the waiting long boats on the day of their departure: in reality they must have driven a half mile further and left far more simply (though also rather perilously) from the landing steps.

Historians consider that slavery on St Helena throughout the early nineteenth-century was less vicious than it was in many places elsewhere, and it is unlikely that an island slave during that period would have been marked by the scars of shackles (under Hudson Lowe's governorship it was further decreed that all children born to slaves from 1818 were to be considered free). There was no post-funeral 'repast' at Longwood House comparable to the one I describe, and Napoleon - not living on, as far as we know, as a ghost – never wrote a series of letters to be found by posterity. Finally, my largest distortion of the truth comes in the final pages of the novel, for Marchand was not left on the island to guard the emperor's body, but returned with the rest of the party to France.

In relation to the whodunit part of the mystery, it is true that Napoleon's body was not embalmed, that it was buried within four coffins, and that when disinterred almost twenty years later, was found to be whole, preserved and 'almost exactly' as it had been when he first died.

The cause of the death of the man who once ruled over 83 million subjects continues to be passionately debated even today, almost two centuries after his last breath. The doctors who conducted the post mortem examination in 1821 found him to have died from stomach cancer (as they do in *Black Rock*), but numerous investigations since then by medical historians have resulted in over 30 new and different diagnoses, as dissimilar as syphilis, scurvy and hepatitis.

Our own generation does have an advantage over the eight doctors who pondered over the mystery in 1821: scientific analysis is far more advanced today. During the five years I spent researching and writing this novel in St Helena, Corsica, Paris and the Rare Books Room of the British Library, my own reading has led me to side with the work of Swedish scientist and poisons expert, Sten Forshufvud, and Canadian historian and former President of the International Napoleonic Society, Ben Weider.

The publication of Marchand's St Helena diary in 1955 was the catalyst for their work. Marchand was vigilant, diligent and observant, and, most importantly, in his role as a valet, he was virtually always around to witness the most intimate moments in the progression of the Emperor's illness: his enemas and emetics, his medicines and new drinks. Napoleon is exasperated in *Black Rock* that Marchand should "detail so laboriously my every mouthful of egg, my every fever and pain," yet it is exactly that detail that allowed a fresh insight into what happened in the final weeks of Napoleon's life. The new information that emerged from Marchand's diary, together with the bizarre circumstances of 1840 (when an unembalmed body emerged fully preserved from a twenty year grave) determined Forshufvud and Weider to combine their skills – of forensic science and Napoleonic scholarship – and to re-examine the death of the emperor with modern investigative tools.

In 1960, Forshufvud analysed hair samples known to have come from Napoleon's head. Like many of his contemporaries exposed to the arsenic-rich glues and dyes of the period, Napoleon had much higher levels of arsenic in his hair than any person would have today. But by taking advantage of new forensic techniques, Forschufvud was able to demonstrate that there were huge peaks and troughs in the levels of arsenic in Napoleon's hair – peaks and troughs consistent with *periodic* arsenic *ingestion*, not *daily* arsenic *absorption*. Hence 'the arsenic in the hair pomade' or the 'arsenic in the green wallpaper' theory – so popular in the 1970s (and echoed in *Black Rock* by references to the lugubrious green walls of the house) – was disproved by his analysis. Poisoning in either manner would have resulted in much lower and more consistent levels of arsenic in the hair.

Sten Forshufvud's initial paper, published in 1961 in *Nature*, was generally derided and his theory (that Napoleon had been poisoned) dismissed as that of a crackpot. In the four decades following, he and Weider went on to track down many more samples of Napoleon's hair, to address criticisms about their methodology, and to subject the hair to different forms of analysis (including nuclear testing and graphite furnace atomic absorption spectroscopy). Luckily for them, Napoleon lived at a time when it was usual to give locks of your hair to your loved ones, and they found many well-authenticated samples. In time, it was not only the Harwell Nuclear Research Laboratory in London that confirmed the toxic levels of arsenic in Napoleon's hair, but also the Federal Bureau of Investigation (FBI), the Louis Pasteur Institute and Europe's leading toxicology centre, the Institute of Legal Medicine. When Scotland Yard investigators reviewed the evidence presented to them by Weider, they confirmed that if comparable arsenic levels were found during a modern investigation, the case would be referred immediately to the criminal prosecution unit.

Weider's and Forshufvud's findings were published in *Assassination at St Helena* (1978), *Assassination at St Helena Revisited* (1995) and in the 1982 *Murder of Napoleon* (co-written by David Hapgood). In all three books, historian Weider also drew upon his vast knowledge of the St Helena primary source literature to move beyond mere hair analysis.

In his research, he points out that Napoleon had 30 of the 34 known symptoms of arsenic poisoning whilst on St Helena; that he was renowned to drink and eat very rapidly because of his impatience with lingering over the pleasures of the table. He points out that although the food eaten at Longwood House was shared by all those living there, Napoleon had his own special wine, the *vin de Constance*, which was imported for him especially from Cape Town and which only he drank; and that Montholon, as sommelier and Head of the Household Stores, would have had full access to that wine. He points out that Napoleon first drank *orgeat* on April 22nd 1821, just 13 days before his death, and that three days later a new case of bitter almonds (the critical active ingredient in *orgeat*) was delivered to Longwood House to assuage the emperor's extreme thirst (also a symptom of arsenic poisoning). He references the fact that on the afternoon of the 3rd of May, according to both Marchand's and Bertrand's diaries, Napoleon was given without his knowledge or consent, 10 grains of calomel (around 40 times the usual dose), and that "shortly afterwards," according to Bertrand, "he fell unconscious. He was completely immobilised . . . he could not even swallow." (Mercury cyanide, which can be created by mixing calomel and *orgeat*, is known to paralyse the voluntary motor functions). He died 48 hours after taking the calomel without regaining consciousness.

Weider and Forshufvud concluded that Napoleon had been poisoned on St Helena, that there was probably a Bourbon sympathiser among his court, and that Montholon – with the connections, the motive, the access and the means – 'probably did it'.

Other theories have, of course, emerged since then. Friends sometimes write to tell me: *It's been proven; he wasn't poisoned: it was stomach cancer . . . it was gonorrhoea . . . it was the climate of St Helena . . . it was Lowe . . . it was the British.* It is unlikely that we will ever all agree. But for my bet, Weider's and Forshufvud's research is the closest that we come to the truth today.

Historian Ben Weider spent 40 years of his life trying to prove his theory, and recognition came from many quarters in the end. During his lifetime he received over 60 awards and honours from more than 20 countries, and became a Knight of the Order of Quebec, a Member of the Order of Canada, a Chevalier of the Legion of Honor, and a Serving Brother of the Order of St. John. He was also nominated for the Nobel Peace prize. On the day he was made Honorary Chief Inspector of the Montreal Police Department for his research into Napoleon's death, Montreal Police Chief, Jacques Duchesneau, described him "as the greatest detective I have ever met."

Moving on to the events of 1840: all of the main figures that return in my Epilogue (Bertrand, Arthur, Gourgaud, Pierron) returned in reality with the exception of Montholon, who could not travel since he was imprisoned at the time for his part in a failed coup to establish Louis-Napoléon on the throne of France (one of the main reasons, surely, to doubt that Montholon was a Bourbon sympathiser, unless, of course, it was a spectacular double-bluff). The party was also joined by other members of the exile (including several who don't feature in my story such as Las Cases, St Denis, Noverraz, Archambault and Coursot). It was actually Santini, Napoleon's usher, who later became the guardian of the Emperor's tomb at Les Invalides.

As Napoleon watches his body being buried in *Black Rock*, he rues that: "All my great works, everything I had done, all the changes I had brought to France and the world, would in their time fade, and not a single law or principle or practice of mine would remain." In fact, he did leave a legacy that still resonates today, not least in the *Code Napoléon* which remains the foundation of so many modern legal systems, with its emphasis on meritocracy, transparency, accountability and freedom of religion. Historian Robert Holtman regards it as one of the few documents that have influenced the entire world. He also left a visual legacy in the millions of trees he planted in long straight avenues all across Europe so that his soldiers could march wherever possible in the shade. *An army marches on his stomach* and *Not tonight, Josephine*, are words of his that live on (even in their distorted forms). His administrative and legal reforms still inspire modernising states, and mathematics would be far harder than it is without his metric system. His battles are part of the curricula in military academies from Saint-Cyr to West Point, and his campaign strategies are taught to new generations of soldiers alongside those of Hannibal and Alexander the Great. The legacy of those battles is also visible throughout Europe in the graveyards that contain the five million or so soldiers and civilians that were killed in the wars that bear his name.

By 1814, Napoleon had come to believe that "a throne is only a board lined with velvet," yet he had painfully longed for a son to continue sitting on his velvet-lined board. His dynasty did not, in fact, cease with the death of his son, Napoleon II, as seemed apparent in 1840, at the end of *Black Rock*. In 1848, his nephew, Louis-Napoléon Bonaparte (who was the child of his step-daughter, Hortense de Beauharnais, and his brother, Louis) was elected President in France's first-ever popular vote. He initiated a *coup d'état* three years later and ascended to the throne of France – on the 48th anniversary of his uncle's coronation – as Napoleon III.

Louis-Napoléon ruled as 'Emperor of the French' for almost 20 years, until defeat by the Prussians in 1870 forced him from the throne. He was the last monarch of France, and he too spent his last years in exile, though not in such a gothic, remote spot as St Helena. He died instead in the homeland of his uncle's greatest enemy: England.

Louise Hoole
Tanzania

LOUISE HOOLE

Acknowledgements

Black Rock was written in many places: in the 45 degree heat of the Karoo desert and in a cold rectory in Oxfordshire; among the ancient peaks of St Helena and during a trance festival in Malawi; in the studious silence of the British Library's Rare Books Room and in a garden of frangipanis and guinea fowls in Dar es Salaam.

For me, this book is infused not so much with those places, but with the people who were around me whilst it was being made. So many of my friends and family members contributed to *Black Rock* by being cheerleaders for my writing, or sharing my passion for St Helena or Napoleon, or engaging in conversations about a strange group of exiles living on a rock in the mid-Atlantic almost two centuries ago.

I am so grateful to my early readers - Chloe Taylor, Elsie Eyakuze, Fiona Bergmann, Fiona Shaw, Lisa María Noudéhou, Jim Blandford, James and Giles Tremayne, Mathew Clayton, Marigold Joy, Pauline Dellar, Robina and John Jacobson, Teal Paynter, Tina Lee, Tina Rose and Walter Bgoya - for their sharp eyes, kind tongues and wise words.

My particular gratitude to my mother and brother for always championing my writing; to Colin for showing me how a good story should be told; to my godmother for always wanting me to be literary; to James, Giles, Soraya and Bruce Tremayne for indulging me in lengthy discussions about centuries-dead dictators; to

Mathew Clayton for the practical support he has given me over the years, and to my writing friends - Abdu Simba, Elsie Eyakuze, Fiona Shaw, James Blandford, Lisa María Noudéhou, Marigold Joy and Omar Mohammed - for their witty and inspiring company, and for making it never seem odd to ask questions like: 'So would it work if I killed him off in the first section, but brought him back as a ghost in chapter two...?"

There are beloved people who, frankly, haven't contributed a word to this text, but who have brought much joy to my life in England, Africa and St Helena: thanks to Angela Tormin, Cherry Walters, Guillaume Barraut, Hannes Esterhazy, Milord Wayne Banks, Nigel Henry, James Tremayne, Jason Rubens, Julian Rumball, Natalia Celani, Sarah Markes, Sarah Scott, Simon Wall, Stedson Stroud, Paulo Smithson, and Ulric Charteris, as well as to les familles Arthur-Lee, Bown, Bergmann, Bush, Corrigan Karimjee, De Steiger Khandwala, Dellar, Francis-Jones, Hamilton, Hoole, Liebchen, Liversidge, Lovett, Main, Skripek, Thorpe and Whitt-Russ. My love and esteem especially to Mum, Colin, John, Jules and my gorgeous nephews, Charlie and Tristan.

On a professional level, I am indebted to Marigold Joy for naming this book in a flash of inspiration in the Pyrénées; to Wayne Banks for designing the stunning cover and creating the first ever font, the Napoleayne, modelled on the Emperor's dying handwriting; to Mathew Clayton for guiding me on legal and industry issues; to Trevor Hearl and Michel Dancoisne-Martineau for their historical knowledge and advice; and to the staff of the British Library and the St Helena Archives for their efficiency and enthusiasm. My special thanks to Lisa María Noudéhou who liked this book enough to want to publish it, and who knows so well how to nudge a writer when needed, to bring out the compliments and biscuits when needed, and to lay down a stern deadline when that too is needed.

Finally, I owe the biggest debt to my parents who made the decision to take my brother and me to St Helena in 1978, and introduced us to the island we fell in love with. Thanks always to Dad for spotting the advert in *The Times* which took us to the island, and started this adventure.

St Helena is a volcanic island, sculpted into its present shape by eruptions that took place around seven million years ago. The mountainous terrain of the island's 47 square miles is extremely varied, ranging from the near-barren cliffs that surround the main town to the lush, ancient ferns of Diana's Peak. St Helena is in the South Atlantic Ocean, at 15° 56' South and 5° 42' West. It was uninhabited when discovered by the Portuguese in 1502.

Lightning Source UK Ltd.
Milton Keynes UK
UKOW04n1257170214

226602UK00001B/1/P